No Place to Hide

When Joe Spearman sees a face from the past, he gets a shock. It's the face of a killer. It is also someone who now has a good deal of influence and power in the little town of Ox Crossing. Someone who won't want his past catching up with him. However, before Joe can do anything about his discovery, the man he has recognized acts quickly and Joe is silenced. Permanently.

It is then up to his old army buddy, Nat Leach, to discover the identity of the person behind Joe's murder. But Nat is pursuing his own personal mission: tracking down the men who slaughtered two members of his family while he was away fighting a war. And he's getting close to finding them, even though they, too, have new identities.

Nat soon learns that he has taken on two perilous quests, and that he could end up like his old army buddy.

Dead.

No Place to Hide

John Davage

A Black Horse Western

ROBERT HALE

© John Davage 2018
First published in Great Britain 2018

ISBN 978-0-7198-2771-6

The Crowood Press
The Stable Block
Crowood Lane
Ramsbury
Marlborough
Wiltshire SN8 2HR

www.bhwesterns.com

Robert Hale is an imprint
of The Crowood Press

PROLOGUE

STOKEWOOD 1859

The card game broke up just after 2 a.m. Martin Benson made his way from the Stokewood Hotel and into the moonlit street of the town. He was unsteady on his feet, but sober enough to know he'd lost four hundred and fifty dollars to his fellow poker players, three regulars who joined him each Friday night at the hotel and to whom he now owed – between them – somewhere close to two thousand dollars.

The three each took rooms at the hotel rather than make the journey to their homes on a Friday night – all of which lay several miles from the town. Two were farmers, the third a rancher. All were cannier poker players than Benson.

He had no intention of going home. Instead he would bed down on the couch in the back room of the estate office. It was something he was doing more often, avoiding the soured atmosphere at the large frame house which

stood a mile outside town. It was two storeys high with dormer windows in the roof and a wide veranda along the front. Built by his father-in-law, Duff Hammond, as a wedding present six years ago, Benson hated it.

Cora, his wife, would be sound asleep in her room. Their childless marriage had long since become little more than a convenience, a sham that fooled no one in Stokewood, including Cora's seventy-year-old father. Duff Hammond was the town's biggest property owner and employer, and its most influential citizen. Too many people owed him either money or favours to openly criticize Cora, even though she was generally considered to be a harridan. People even expressed sympathy for her drunkard of a husband.

Benson was Hammond's 'estate manager', an overblown title for a job that was little more than an office clerk and rent collector, and well below the forty-five-year-old's capabilities. So Benson felt no guilt about creaming off some of the money due to Hammond by careful adjustment of the accounts. But even that didn't provide enough to clear his gambling debts.

The estate office was a low, flat-roofed adobe building. It stood on the opposite side of the street from the hotel. As Benson approached it, he saw a light in the back room, overlooking the alleyway at the side of the building. He blinked several times to be sure it wasn't the whiskey playing tricks on him – but no, there was definitely a flickering light, as if from a lamp. And at the rear of the building he could make out the shadowy shape of the rump of a horse.

'What the. . . ?'

Benson hesitated at the Main Street end of the alleyway and considered his options. There was a .45 in the drawer of his desk, but otherwise he was unarmed. For a brief moment he considered waking the town marshal, but in the end decided to leave him to his slumbers.

It was a decision that would have fateful consequences.

Fourteen-year-old Joey Spearman woke with bellyache.

'Pesky gooseberries!' he muttered to himself. 'Should've listened to Annie, she told me they weren't ripe.'

Annie was the wife of Judah Jones, Stokewood's blacksmith and liveryman, for whom Joey had worked since the day he had quit going to school. The gooseberries had been for bottling, but Joey hadn't been able to resist wolfing down a handful in spite of Annie's warning. And now he was paying for it.

Another sharp pain attacked his gut, and he felt an urgent need of the privy. It meant crawling from his cot in the tiny room he occupied in the loft over the livery and making his way in the dark to the little building out back. Judah and his wife had a modest little house five hundred yards away up the side street, so there was nobody to disturb.

Joey had no idea of the time, though he reckoned it was the early hours of the morning. Stumbling out of the back door of the livery into the moonlit yard, he was only half aware of a light across the side street. It came from a room at the back of Hammond's estate office, but the increasing urgency to empty his bowels meant that it hardly registered in Joey's consciousness. However, the piebald horse

7

standing at the rear of the building did register, because Joey, who had tended to most horses in the town at one time or another, recognized it as belonging to Jabal Hawley. But such was the urgency of his nocturnal mission that he gave it only a passing thought.

Yanking the privy door shut behind him and plunging himself into near total darkness, he pulled up his nightshirt.

Benson decided to avoid fumbling with keys and unlocking the front entrance of the estate office. Instead, he went up the alleyway to the back door – and immediately recognized the distinctive piebald horse waiting patiently for its owner. An owner Benson knew only too well.

'Hawley!' Martin muttered to himself.

It was not a complete surprise. Jabal Hawley had made threats to Duff Hammond on more than one occasion, threats of violence, even arson.

The back door had been forced and stood partly open. Cautiously, Benson eased it further ajar. It led directly into the lamp-lit room where Benson could see the back of Hawley as the latter tried to open the box-shaped safe which had been set into the wall. A coal oil lamp stood on a small table next to the desk, throwing shadows across the room. Papers were strewn across the top of the desk where Benson had been working on them the day before.

Benson pushed the door open wide.

'The safe needs a key, Hawley.'

The other man swung round, uttering an oath and drawing a pistol from his waistband. '*Benson!*'

'Hey, ease off!' Benson said, putting up his hands. 'No need for guns.' He avoided looking at the desk drawer where he kept the .45, calculating the odds of reaching it before Hawley shot him. He decided they weren't good.

'What the hell are you doin' here at this time?' Hawley growled.

'I was planning a peaceful night over there,' Benson answered, pointing towards the couch standing along one wall.

Hawley snorted. 'Too bad.' He nodded at the safe. 'You got a key for this?'

'No, 'fraid not.' It was a lie. Benson could feel the bunch of keys in his jacket pocket. 'Hammond keeps it.'

'Guess I'll have to shoot out the lock then,' Hawley said.

'Hold on,' Benson said. 'I think he keeps a spare key in the desk. Want me to take a look?'

'OK, but take it slow. One wrong move an' you're dead.'

'What's this, taking some recompense for your farm?' Benson asked, moving slowly towards the desk.

'Too damn right I am,' Hawley snarled. 'You know as well as I do that Hammond was responsible for burnin' my corn crop an' forcin' the bank to foreclose on my mortgage. So I'm takin' whatever's in this safe an' gettin' out of this damn town pronto. Think I'll set me a little fire afore I leave, too. Kinda tit for tat, don't you reckon?'

Benson had reached the desk. 'The key's in the centre drawer.'

'Open it real slow.'

Benson eased open the drawer, stretched out a hand and grasped the Peacemaker. . . .

*

Joey heard the echo of the two gunshots from inside the privy, but he was still squatting and voiding the contents of his bowels, and so in no position to investigate. Besides, although Stokewood was a generally peaceable town, a gunshot or two at any time of day or night was not uncommon.

'Another gun-happy drunk using the sign outside the saloon for target practice,' Joey decided.

It was a full five minutes before he felt able to emerge into the night again, his stomach pains having eased somewhat.

At first he was puzzled by the sudden brightness. Moments later, he realized the glow came from flames inside the estate office.

'Jeeze! It's on fire!'

And the blaze had taken hold, Joey could see that through the back window and the open back door. It was then that he remembered Hawley's piebald horse that had been standing at the end of the alleyway.

It was gone.

It was another fifteen minutes before Joey Spearman had roused enough people from their sleep to tackle the blaze, and by then it was far too late to save anything inside the adobe building.

And it was much later that the town marshal found the charred remains of a body amongst the ashes, alongside an empty safe.

CHAPTER 1

OX CROSSING 1870

Angie Smith rolled off the bed and gathered up her wrap to cover her naked body. Joe Spearman had already pulled on his pants and denim shirt and was standing barefoot at the window of her room, which was shut tight against the chilly grey February morning. The room was on the first floor of Angie's boarding house, which, as everyone in Ox Crossing knew, doubled as a brothel. It also provided cheaper accommodation than either of the town's two hotels, besides the added bonus of the delights that Angie and her girls could offer.

It was the first time Joe had availed himself of these pleasures since arriving in town three days before. In fact he had barely acquainted himself with any of the other amenities the town had on offer, having spent the first day sleeping off the effects of a hard six-day ride to get here, the second getting a bath and shave at the barber shop before becoming involved in a game of faro at the Silver

Buck saloon, and this morning enjoying his landlady's company.

'Hope I didn't disappoint,' Angie said, coming alongside him at the window and putting an arm around his neck. She was thirty years old – five years older than Joe – plump verging on fat, hair the colour of over-ripe corn, and a generous mouth painted bright red. 'Although judgin' by your *enthusiasm* . . .'

'Mm?' Joe was preoccupied with something in the street below.

Angie peered out of the window. 'Somethin' goin' on down there? Somethin' caught your interest?'

'What? No, not 'xactly.' He frowned. 'I'm probably wrong. It's just . . .'

'Wrong about what?' Angie asked.

She could see nothing out of the ordinary happening in Main Street. Just people going about their business, visiting the mercantile or Freda's eating place, a small huddle of men talking together outside the bank, a rider dismounting from his horse and tethering it to the hitching rail outside the Silver Buck. She recognized him as Luke Trey, trouble-shooter for Cleve Connor, owner of the Circle C ranch. Connor was one of the little gathering outside the bank, but Trey made no move in his direction. Instead he entered the saloon.

'See somebody you know?' Angie persisted.

'Maybe,' Joe said. 'Difficult to say. Eleven years is a long time. People change.'

'In appearance, maybe,' Angie said. 'Deep down, they're often the same ornery critters.'

Joe laughed. 'That's what my old army buddy Nat

12

always said.'

'This *hombre* you reckon you've seen, did he do somethin' he shouldn't have?'

'If it's the same guy, he burned out a buildin' and
escaped with the contents of the safe, as well as killin'
someone. But I could be wrong. I was just a fourteen-
year-old kid at the time.'

After Joe left to go up to his eyrie on the top floor – the
cheapest room in the house – Angie continued to assess
the scene below. The only remaining players in the little
street drama were the five men in conversation outside
the bank. Apart from Cleve Connor, she identified Lyle
Walker, Howard Ellis, Otis Bream and Sheriff Chesney
Francome.

Angie could guess what they were discussing. It would be
the forthcoming spring mayoral election. Both Walker
and Ellis were standing for election – in Ellis's case re-
election – and would probably be canvassing support
from the other three.

'Politics,' Angie muttered to herself. 'Huh!'

And she shrugged off the wrap and reached for her
chemise.

In his room, Joe was digging amongst his things for an
ancient newspaper report from the *Stokewood Times*, dated
October, 1859. The creased and browned cutting had trav-
elled with him for eleven years, all through the War, and
his years of drifting since the conflict. Why? Joe would
have been hard pressed to give an exact reason, other
than the fact that it represented a significant, albeit brief,
moment in his boyhood when he had been the centre of

attention, when for once people had listened to what he'd had to say. It hadn't happened often since then.

He had only ever shown the cutting to one other person: his confederate army buddy, Nat Leach, whom he had lost track of in the months after the War when Nat headed home to Arizona and his folks' farm.

Now Joe spread the cutting out on the washstand and cast his eyes over the familiar words:

Murder in the Small Hours

Martin Benson, estate manager and son-in-law of the town's most prominent citizen, Mr Duff Hammond, was shot to death in the early hours of Saturday morning at the Hammond Estate Office. The killer then set fire to the building before escaping with the contents of the wall safe – approximately $900.

Fourteen-year-old Joey Spearman, spotting the fire after making a middle-of-the-night call of nature, alerted the night porter in the Stokewood Hotel, and as many neighbours he could rouse from their slumbers. But alas to no avail. The fire had taken too strong a hold, and in spite of valiant efforts by a bucket line of fire-fighting townspeople, the entire innards of the building were destroyed. Benson's charred remains were discovered only after the building was safe to enter.

Joey Spearman was able to give a strong pointer to the identity of the killer. Joey, whose job is to tend horses at Judah Jones' livery and knows most people's horses in Stokewood, recognized the piebald animal standing outside the rear entrance to the estate office before the fire and which had disappeared afterwards.

'That horse belonged to Mr Hawley,' Jocy told town marshal Jessop confidently.

And subsequent investigations by the marshal seemed to confirm that thirty-eight-year-old Jabal Hawley was the culprit. The shack he had been living in since losing his farm was empty of his belongings and had all the signs of a hurried departure. It is also known that Hawley blamed Duff Hammond for the burning of his corn crop and the subsequent mortgage foreclosure, which meant losing his farm. Hawley has also been heard to threaten revenge on Mr Hammond, including arson as a form of poetic justice.

There is a $1,000 reward for any information that results in the capture of Jabal Hawley.

Joe folded the newspaper cutting, sitting in thoughtful silence for several minutes. $1,000 for any information. He could sure use a thousand dollars. Funds were getting low. But he had to be certain. He looked at the picture – an artist's sketch – of Jabal Hawley's face that was at the centre of the newspaper report. It was the same sketch he'd seen on law dodgers at various times over the interceding years. It was a poor likeness. The sort of face that would have fitted a hundred men. Joey thought back to the face he'd seen from Angie's window. And gradually he became more certain his notion had been right.

15

$1,000! Or maybe the man he'd seen would be pre-
pared to pay Joe even more to keep quiet. Of course he
might be minded to ensure Joe's silence about his new
identity by putting a bullet in Joe's back.

Joe suddenly felt in need of a strong drink.

Three days later, Joe left the Silver Buck saloon just before
midnight to make his way back to his room in Angie's
establishment, having won twenty-four dollars playing
poker and having drunk rather more whiskey than was
wise. Which was why he failed to notice he was being followed until it was too late.

Suddenly a hand twisted him round and shoved him in
the chest so that he fell backwards and lay sprawled
amongst the dirt and detritus of a dark alleyway next to
the saddle shop.

'What the. . . ?' he began, before a blade was shoved
between his ribs and into his heart. It was done with the
precision of someone who had done it many times before.

His attacker leaned over him and withdrew the knife.
Joe stared up at him through glassy pain-filled eyes, blood
trickling from the corner of his mouth.

'Why. . . ?' he asked through ragged breath.

'You asked too many questions,' his assailant answered
after a moment.

But Joe didn't hear him. He would never hear anyone
again.

CHAPTER 2

Nat Leach brought his chestnut gelding to a halt, screwed up his eyes against the April sunshine and took in the mid-afternoon quiet of Ox Crossing's sparsely populated Main Street. Siesta time, he decided. He was conscious of two old-timers sitting on the boardwalk outside the mercantile looking him over. What they saw was a tall, lean man in his mid-twenties, brown hair worn slightly long and a square chin in need of a shave. He wore denim pants tucked into cracked leather boots, a check shirt and a creased tan Stetson. Besides his saddlebags, the stock of a Winchester poked out of a scabbard at the right side of his horse. His right hand rested casually on his hip, within easy reach of a holstered Colt .45.

Nat gigged his mount forward, having noticed the open doors of a livery down the street. And a few yards further on the sign for a modest, and hopefully inexpensive, hotel. A little while later, his horse stabled, he carried his saddlebags and Winchester to the hotel and secured himself a room.

'Number eight, first floor,' the clerk told him. He was a

short, skinny man with greasy hair, hollowed cheeks and an unhealthy pallor. He handed Nat a key.

'Thanks,' Nat said. 'Tell me, does the name Travis Newton mean anything to you? Somebody local, maybe?'

The little man shook his head. 'Nope. I don't know everybody, of course. You could try asking Ted Norton at the livery.'

'I already did. Name meant nothing to him either.' Nat nodded towards the open guest book and the lines of scrawled signatures.

'Somebody passing through, maybe?'

'Maybe,' the clerk said. 'Don't remember the name, but you're welcome to have a look.' He pushed the book across the desk towards Nat.

'Thanks,' Nat said again. He flipped through the pages but drew a blank.

'You got a special reason you're lookin' for this Newton *hombre*?' the clerk asked.

Nat gave a humourless smile. 'Yeah, it's kinda special,' he said.

Half an hour later he made his way along the street until he found a barber shop. There he took a long bath to soak off the grime of his journey before planting himself in the barber's chair and indicating he needed a shave.

For a time, he was the only patron as he fended off the barber's questions.

'Just passing through or planning to stay awhile?'

'Not sure,' Nat said.

'Come far?'

'Far enough.'

'What's your line of business?'

'This and that.'

The barber finished lathering Nat's face and took up the razor. He was puzzled by Nat's reticence. Was the stranger on the run from the law? Judging by his appearance when he'd come in, he'd been riding for several days. And he certainly smelled sweeter after that bath.

At that moment the door opened and a short stubby barrel of a man entered. He had virtually no hair, wizened features and wore round wire-framed eyeglasses. Nat guessed him to be in his seventies.

'Morning, Gabe,' the barber greeted him.

'Morning, Tom,' the newcomer replied. He gave Nat the once-over then held out a liver-spotted hand. 'Howdy. Welcome to Ox Crossing. I'm Gabe Crighton, editor of *The Weekly Crossing*.'

'That's our local rag,' the barber informed Nat. 'Mostly gossip, but you get some news as well. Right now it's all about this month's mayoral election. Gabe can probably tell you who's going to win.'

'Not so,' the editor said. 'Could be either of the candidates. Guess Howard Ellis has got the edge, him being the present mayor, but Lyle Walker will give him a run for his money.'

There was an awkward silence for several minutes, then Nat said, 'Either of you know or heard of a man called Travis Newton?'

The barber shook his head. 'Can't say I have. How about you, Gabe? You know just about everybody in this town, and you've lived here longer than me.'

Gabe Crighton thought for a moment. 'Not a name I

know. You got a particular reason for finding the man?'

'Yeah, I've got a reason,' Nat replied.

The other two waited for him to elaborate. Then, when it was clear this wasn't going to happen, Gabe said, 'I didn't catch your name, mister.'

'I didn't throw it,' Nat said, wiping the remnants of shaving soap from his jaw after the barber finished working with the razor. 'But it's Nat Leach.'

'Listen, don't take offence,' the editor said. 'It's just that we don't get many strangers in this town, Ox Crossing being a bit off the beaten track.'

'Last one who came ended up with a knife in his chest,' the barber said, chuckling. 'He's on Boot Hill now.'

'That so? They get the killer?' Nat asked.

Gabe and the barber exchanged a look.

'Nope,' Gabe said. 'But then, our workshy sheriff didn't look very hard, isn't that right, Tom?'

The barber avoided their eyes. 'Not for me to say,' he said. 'I run a business here and it don't pay to upset folks if I want to keep running it.'

'Especially not Cleve Connor, right?' Gabe prodded.

The barber didn't reply.

'You reckon this Connor did the killing?' Nat said.

'Not really,' Gabe said. 'Anyway, if Connor *had* wanted Spearman dead he would have paid somebody to do the dirty deed. Connor likes to keep his hands clean.'

'Spearman?' Nat said quickly. Some of the colour went out of his newly shaved face.

'That was the kid's name,' Gabe said. 'Joe Spearman. You reckon you know – knew – him? It's not a common name.'

'What was he like?' Nat asked.

'About your age, early to mid-twenties. Medium height, reddish-brown hair. I never actually spoke to him. He was only here four or five days before he was killed.'

'Had a room at Angie's,' the barber said.

'That's the local whorehouse,' Gabe said. 'Besides the usual facilities, Angie lets out a few rooms. Did you know Spearman?'

'Reckon I did,' Nat replied. He looked shocked. 'We were army buddies for best part of the War. In fact he saved my life on one occasion. Killed a Union sniper who was about to put a bullet in me.'

'So you kinda owe him,' Gabe said.

'I sure do,' Nat said. 'We lost touch after the conflict. I went home to my family farm. Joe said he planned to drift for a year or so. Got a hankering for travelling.'

'He had no family?' Gabe asked.

'Joe's parents died of a fever within weeks of one another when he was a kid,' Nat said. 'That's when he quit school and got a job in a livery.' He frowned. 'Seems odd he riled somebody enough to get himself murdered – Joe was always a friendly guy.'

Gabe nodded. 'It was a mystery, all right.'

Nat looked thoughtful. 'Seems I've got another reason for lingering a while in Ox Crossing. I'd like to find out more.'

'The kid hardly spoke to anyone 'cepting Angie and Wilf, the barkeep at the Silver Buck,' Gabe said.

'Maybe I'll have a word with them,' Nat said.

'You said Spearing's murder is *another* reason,' Gabe said. 'So you aren't just passing through. Was finding this

21

Newton *hombre* your first reason for coming here?'

'Could be,' Nat said, evasively. He stood up. 'Right now, though, I need food. Where's a good place to eat?'

'Freda's eating house, a couple of blocks down on the corner,' the barber said.

After Nat left, Gabe took the place he had vacated in the barber's chair. 'Kinda tight-lipped about his reasons for wanting to find the Newton character, wasn't he?' he said to the barber.

The other man gave a short laugh. 'But that's the sort of challenge you like, Gabe.'

After demolishing a plate of lamb stew, fried potatoes and cabbage, together with two mugs of strong black coffee, Nat indicated he'd like a third. Freda waddled across the room with the coffee pot, breathing heavily. Beads of sweat dotted her brow. She wiped it with her apron.

Nat posed the question he'd been asking in the hotel and barber shop.

'Nobody I know,' Freda told him. She addressed the three other diners – a young cowhand and the two old-timers Nat had seen earlier. 'You ever heard of a Travis Newton?'

The reply was three negative grunts.

'Sorry, mister,' Freda said.

'How about Joe Spearman? Did he ever eat here?'

'The fellah who got himself killed? Yeah, he ate here a coupla times. Nice enough young guy. Must've upset somebody, though.'

'Any idea who?'

Freda shook her head. 'You know him?'

'Yeah, he was a good friend.'

'You could try talkin' to Angie Smith,' the cowhand suggested from across the room. 'She an' he spent some time together, if you know what I mean.'

'Thanks, I was planning to,' Nat said. He swallowed the last of his coffee and made for the door.

A few minutes after Nat left, a tall, angular man with thinning grey hair and the complexion of a heavy drinker entered the eating house. A silver star pinned to his leather vest announced the fact that he was Ox Crossing's lawman.

'Afternoon, Ches,' Freda greeted him.

Sheriff Chesney Francome gave a little wave of the hand and sank unsteadily into a chair by the nearest table. As Freda approached him, she detected the smell of whiskey and stale tobacco.

'Saw some critter leavin' here a few minutes ago,' Francome said. 'Any idea who he is?'

'He didn't say,' Freda said. 'An' I didn't ask. You wantin' anythin' to eat? There's some lamb stew left.'

Francome grimaced. 'Maybe just coffee. So we don't know who he is or what he's doin' here?'

'He was askin' about the young guy who got himself killed,' the cowhand said. 'Seems he was a friend.'

The sheriff looked across at the other table. 'That so?'

'Still don't know who killed him, do we sheriff?' one of the old-timers said, a twinkle in his eye.

'Prob'ly never will, Sam,' his companion said with an exaggerated, rueful shake of his head. 'In spite of all the effort our good sheriff has put into investigatin' the crime.'

Sam gave a big theatrical sigh. 'Guess you're right, Aaron.'

The colour of Francome's face turned an even deeper shade of puce, but before he could answer his elderly critics, Freda cut him short.

'He was also askin' about a Travis Newton,' she said quickly, forestalling an argument with the old-timers. 'Not that it's a name any of us ever heard before. Now I'll get you some fresh coffee, Ches.'

She turned and tottered off to the kitchen.

And by doing so, missed seeing the colour drain from Sheriff Francome's face.

CHAPTER 3

The Silver Buck was like a hundred other saloons Nat had been in. A long bar, lines of bottles behind it; a scattering of tables, a few covered in felt for card players, others plain wood with three or four wooden chairs around them. There were a dozen or so men at the tables and four men leaning against the bar counter.

Nat ordered himself a beer from the barkeep. 'Guess you'd be Wilf,' he said.

'That's me,' the barkeep replied, placing a foaming glass of beer in front of Nat. He was a short, plump man with thinning hair that had been carefully combed across an otherwise bald head.

'I'm told you had a conversation or two with an army buddy of mine,' Nat said.

'Really? Who would that be?'

'Joe Spearman.'

The barkeep suddenly became intent on polishing the empty glass in his hand. 'That so?'

'Yeah, it is. Mind telling me what you talked about?'

'Nothin' particular.'

'Did he mention what brought him to town?'

'Nope. I got the impression he was just another drifter.'

'You get many drifters passing through?' Nat asked after a moment.

'Some.' The barkeep finally met Nat's eye. 'Guess you'd be one, wouldn't you?'

'Sort of.' Nat drank a long draught of his beer. 'Got any ideas about Joe's killing? You see him upset anyone, or get into an argument?'

The barkeep shook his head. 'He started askin' questions a day or so afore he was killed.'

Nat was suddenly alert. 'What kind of questions, Wilf?'

'About how long some of the local people had lived here. Where they'd come from. That sorta thing. Not that I could tell him much, I've only lived here a coupla years myself.'

'Anybody particular he was curious about?'

Wilf put the glass on the shelf behind him, leaned against the bar counter and lowered his voice. 'Well, that's the strange thing. He seemed careful *not* to give the impression he was askin' about any one person. As though admittin' to bein' interested in one particular man might act as a kinda warnin' signal. Might ring an alarm bell for that somebody.'

'But you didn't get any ideas about who that person was.'

' 'Fraid not.' Wilf suddenly looked beyond Nat to the batwing doors. 'But here's somebody who your friend might've confided in. That's Angie.'

Nat turned to see a comfortably round woman with corn-coloured hair and a world-weary look on her face crossing the room. She was followed closely by a hollow-cheeked *hombre* with a knife-slash of a mouth and bushy black eyebrows. Nat put him in his mid-thirties.

'Who's the guy behind her?' Nat asked.

'Luke Trey,' Wilf answered. 'Nasty piece of work. Don't go messin' with him, mister.'

The man in question stretched out a hand and grabbed Angie's arm, stalling her. 'Not so fast, Angie,' he rasped. 'Let me buy you a drink, then we can go to your place for a little . . . entertainment.'

Angie pulled her arm free. 'Nothing doing, Luke,' she said. 'And you can stay away from my girls. They don't like the way you rough them up when you have your way with them.'

Trey's expression darkened. 'Too bad,' he snarled. 'I'll treat a whore any damn way I please, an' . . .'

'*No!*' Angie faced him with a scowl. 'Go near any of my girls an' I'll be having words with your boss about it. Cleve Connor is a . . . client of mine, and he wouldn't take kindly to his chief henchman upsetting me or any of my girls.'

Trey stared at her for a full ten seconds, then stormed off to one of the tables in the corner of the room. '*Bitch!*' he muttered. Then yelled to the barkeep, 'Bring me a bottle of red-eye, an' make it quick!'

The other occupants of the saloon seemed to heave a collective sigh as the little drama ended without bloodshed. The card players went back to their games. All of them pointedly avoided looking in Luke Trey's direction.

Wilf took the bottle and a glass across to Trey's table, then beckoned Angie across to the bar where Nat was standing, nursing his beer. 'Gent here would appreciate a word, Angie.' He looked at Nat. 'I didn't get your name.'

'Nat Leach,' Nat said, holding out a hand to Angie.

She took it with a look of surprise. 'Well, I'll be. . . .'

'What?' Nat said.

'You're the army buddy Joe Spearman mentioned a few times,' Angie said.

'He did?'

'Sure did.' She held out a hand to shake.

Nat reciprocated. 'Well, it's Joe I wanted to talk to you about.'

'Sure,' Angie said. 'Wilf, give me a brandy.'

'Let me get that,' Nat said. 'And pour me another beer, Wilf.' He tossed some coins on the bar counter.

'Get a table, an' I'll bring 'em across,' Wilf said.

They found a table at the opposite corner to where Luke Trey was sitting. The latter followed them with his eyes as they sat opposite one another. A minute or two later Wilf brought their drinks.

'You planning on staying in town a while?' Angie asked.

'Maybe. Tell me exactly how Joe was killed,' Nat said after the barkeep had gone away. 'All I've heard is that he got a knife in the chest. Where? When?'

Angie sipped her drink, then said, 'As to where, it was in an alleyway between the saddle shop and the bakery. As to when, it was a night back in February. Joe had been here in the saloon, playing poker with three other men. He left just before midnight, so I was told, to make his way back to my – er – boarding house. It's a hundred yards or so down the street. The two-storey house, with the room in the roof. I say "room", it's not much more than a cupboard. I let Joe have it for a dollar a night.'

Nat chuckled. 'That's less than I'm paying the livery-man to stable my horse. You sure weren't out to make money from my pal.'

'I liked him,' Angie said. 'Besides, it's actually the only room I rent out now. I used to rent out more, but the three other bedrooms, including mine, are used for – well – something a little more profitable.'

'It's OK,' Nat said. 'I've heard. Even so, it's a nice house, if it's the one I'm thinking of. How come. . . ?' He hesitated. 'Well, I guess it's none of my business.'

'How come I can afford to own a place like that?' She took a sip of brandy before continuing. 'A few years back I was the – companion of a businessman, back in Kansas. He was a widower, and when he died he left most of his money to me. It wasn't a fortune, but it was enough for me to leave the wagging tongues of the town behind and set up here. Buying the house took nearly all the money, so I had to come up with a way of making an income.' She looked straight at Nat, challenging him to air his disapproval.

He just shrugged. 'We do what we have to do. Anyways, we've strayed off the subject. We were talking about Joe's murder. How come his body was found in the alleyway?'

'Nobody can be sure, but it's likely he was followed from the saloon or maybe lured into the alleyway by someone – the killer – calling out for help. There would've been no light, 'cepting that from the moon. Joe would just have seen a shadow.'

'Should've been more careful.'

'His body was found next morning.'

'And nobody heard him being attacked?'

29

Angie shook her head. 'Most folk would've been asleep at that time.'

'Yeah, that figures.'

At this point, Luke Trey rose from the table where he'd been sitting and started to walk towards the batwings. Then he stopped, looked in Angie's direction, and made his way over to their table.

Without taking his gaze from Angie, he spoke to Nat. 'Seein' as you're a stranger in town, mister, I reckon I should warn you about this old whore. She's a tease, that's what she is. Likes to get a man all hot an' randy, then cries rape! Dirty little slut deserves. . .' He turned to Angie and raised his left hand, as if to give her a back-hander.

Nat was out of his chair in a flash, grabbing the other man's arm. Trey's right hand went toward his holster but Nat hit him hard in the stomach, then followed through with a blow to the jaw. Trey went backwards, falling on to a table which splintered as he and it hit the floor. For a second time, Trey went for his gun, but again Nat was ahead of him. His .45 was out of its holster and the crackle of the gunshot seemed to happen simultaneously. Trey yelled as blood appeared on his right hand when the bullet found its target, and his .45 spun across the floor as it slipped from his grasp.

Cursing, Trey scrambled to his feet. He reached out to reclaim his weapon.

'Leave it!' Nat said, still holding his Peacemaker. 'You can collect it from the sheriff's office later. Now, get the hell out of here.'

Slowly, Trey got to his feet, a burning hatred in his eyes. He backed off towards the doors, pausing at the batwings to look back at Nat. 'You're a dead man, mister, whoever you are,' he said. Then he was gone.

Nat re-holstered his six-gun, scooped up the other man's weapon and reclaimed his seat.

'You've made an enemy there,' Angie told him. 'And it was my fault. I'm sorry.'

Nat shrugged. 'Don't worry about it. Unlike Joe, I'll be watching my back. Speaking of which, I don't suppose it could've been that critter who killed him?'

'Very possibly,' Angie said.

'Did Joe ever get into an argument with the ornery cuss?'

'Not as far as I know,' Angie said. 'Anyway, Trey works for Cleve Connor, who owns a big spread a mile or two outside of town. He only takes orders from Cleve.'

'Could it have been Connor who Joe upset or threatened in some way?' Nat said.

'As far as I know, Joe never even spoke to Connor,' Angie replied.

'Connor's a name I heard earlier, in the barber shop. Sounded like he's a man of some influence around here.'

'You could say that. There are three or four people in this town who, between them, own most of the property in Ox Crossing. Most townsfolk pay them rent or are repaying them loans.'

'Doesn't sound healthy.' Nat drained the remains of his foamy brew. 'Another drink?'

'No thanks,' Angie said. 'Listen, why don't you come back to the house? I've got something of Joe's that I've been wondering what to do with.'

'You have?'

31

'Yes, it's something which just *might* be a clue to his killing.'

'Lead on,' Nat said.

CHAPTER 4

Cleve Connor sat in a leather-backed swivel chair behind a large walnut desk. A cigar moved back and forth between his teeth as he listened to the panicky voice of the man standing on the other side of the desk.

'I tell you, Cleve, he's trouble.' Sheriff Francome shuffled from foot to foot, twirling his hat in his hands.

'If he is, we'll deal with it,' Connor said. He drew deeply on his cigar and let out a stream of smoke. 'He definitely mentioned the name Newton, you say.'

Francome nodded. 'Travis Newton. An' we both know who. . .'

'Yeah, yeah, we do. Just stay calm and let's see what happens.'

Connor looked older than his forty-nine years, his thick hair and bushy beard almost completely grey, but otherwise he was tall and muscular with steely grey eyes that seemed to look into your soul when he was listening to you.

He was a rich man, having made his money after the

War by winning a silver mine in a game of cards. Its previous owner had run out of cash and, after foolishly letting slip to Connor over a game of faro that the mine was worth investing in, promptly 'lost' it to Connor. Even more foolishly, he had (rightly) accused Cleve of cheating and received a bullet in the head for his pains.

Some eighteen months later, after the mine had finally played out, Cleve Connor landed up in Ox Crossing, and with some of his ill-gotten fortune, bought the Circle C ranch. Since then, by dubious and often downright illegal means, he had managed to acquire several other properties in the town, mostly by intimidating their owners or calling in their loans. It was what had happened to him, at another time in another place, before the War. So he had learned the lesson and now *he* was the one who called in the loans. And you didn't argue with Cleve Connor. If you did, it was likely as not you would end up being work for the local undertaker.

He studied the man in front of him. The two men had met during the War and somehow Francome had tagged on to the stronger man's coat tails after the conflict was over. But though a weak character, he had proved useful to Connor on more than one occasion. Now Francome owed his job as sheriff to Connor, the latter having persuaded (more accurately brow-beaten) the townsfolk that Francome was the right man for the job. Unfortunately those same townsfolk had soon discovered Francome's deficiencies – and not least that he was 'Connor's man'.

Francome finished twirling his hat and put it on his head. 'I'll get back to town then, J . . . er, Cleve, an'. . . .'

'Hell!' Connor exclaimed. 'You nearly did it again, you stupid bastard! How many times do I have to tell you never to call me by that name! One of these days you'll use it in front of somebody who gets curious.'

'Sorry! Sorry, Cleve.' Francome backed away.

After the sheriff had gone, Connor remained seated for a full fifteen minutes, deep in thought. So who was this stranger who was asking questions? How much did he know? He would need to find out.

Meanwhile, one thing was becoming clear. The loose-lipped Francome was becoming a liability. A positive danger when he was nervous, as he was now. Maybe it was time for a change of sheriff.

Angie led Nat into a small room on the ground floor of her house. It was a room she used as an office. On the way into the building, in a kind of lobby, Nat had been confronted with three rouge-cheeked, peroxide-haired females sitting on a *chaise longue*. All three had looked up hopefully at Nat's entrance, only to be disappointed as they noted Angie's shake of the head.

'Business kinda slow?' Nat asked, with a sly grin.

Angie gave him a withering look but said nothing. Instead, she went to a small oak desk, sat down in the chair behind it, then unlocked a drawer and took out a square envelope. From the envelope she withdrew a sheet of newsprint.

'Joe didn't have many belongings,' she said. 'And those he did have the undertaker sold, together with his horse, to cover the cost of his funeral and to pay the liveryman for the care of his animal whilst it was there.'

35

Nat gestured towards the newsprint. 'What's that?'

Angie flattened the paper out on the desk and turned it round so that Nat could read it. 'I rescued it from Joe's things before the undertaker could throw it away as rubbish. I figured if Joe thought it was worth carrying around with him – you'll see it's dated eleven years ago – then it might be important. Then, after I read it, I remembered something Joe said a few days before he died and that got me thinking.'

'What was that? What did Joe say?'

'Read the newspaper report first, then I'll tell you.'

Nat perched on the corner of the desk and picked up the cutting. He started reading and his frown deepened the more he read.

'Interesting,' he said after he'd finished. 'Obviously the "Joey" is Joe. Not that Joey was a name he ever used after he grew up. It was always "call me Joe, I'm not a kid".'

'Joe was all man, I can vouch for that,' Angie said. Then coloured a little, realizing what she'd inferred.

Nat smiled. 'I'll bet you can. Now what was it Joe said that got you thinking?'

'It was after we'd – well, you know. Joe was standing by the window of my room, looking down into Main Street. Something, or *somebody* must've caught his eye because he became distracted. "See somebody you know?" I asked him. "Maybe," he said. "Difficult to say. Eleven years is a long time. People change." Anyway, at first he seemed puzzled, then kinda excited.' Angie nodded at the cutting. 'Anyway, it was the date on the newspaper that started me wondering. 1859. Eleven years ago. The same amount of time Joe had said about people changing.'

'Hang on,' Nat said. 'Are you saying the person Joe saw out of your bedroom window could've been the man mentioned in the picture in this report?'

'Jabal Hawley. Yes, I am. Otherwise why would he have got so excited? There was a $1,000 reward for Hawley, and I expect there still is.'

'So who was in the street that day?' Nat said. 'Can you remember?'

'Sure I can.' Angie ticked them off on her fingers. 'Cleve Connor, Lyle Walker, Howard Ellis, Otis Bream an' Sheriff Francome. They were talking in a little huddle outside the bank. Oh, and Luke Trey went into the saloon. There were a few other people, women, a couple of kids, two or three old timers.'

Nat read part of the report again then looked at Hawley's picture. 'It says here Hawley was thirty-eight years old. That would make him forty-nine now. How old are those men you've just mentioned, and do any of them look anything like the guy in the picture?'

'As to whether they look like Hawley, well no. But like Joe said, people change. They get fatter, grow beards or moustaches, lose some of their hair. I don't know the exact ages of the six, but Luke Trey is probably a bit too young and Lyle Walker would be too old. But any of the other four *could* be in their late forties.'

'Have you shown this to anybody else?' Nat asked.

'No. Although I've been thinking of letting Gabe Crighton take a look at it. He's editor of our local paper.'

'I know, I've met him.'

'Well, I was wondering what would happen if I let Gabe write up some sort of article in *The Weekly Crossing* about the cutting. Whether it might smoke out this Jabal Hawley, make him do something foolish that identified him. That way we might find Joe's killer.'

Nat nodded. 'It's a thought. OK, let's do it. Let's go to the newspaper office. And on the way I'll drop Luke Trey's six-shooter in at the sheriff's, like I promised him.'

'OK,' Angie said.

'By the way, ever heard of a man called Travis Newton?'

Angie thought for a moment, then shook her head. 'No, can't say I have. Why?'

'Tell you later maybe,' Nat said.

Deputy Chap Fancy was making himself a fresh pot of coffee when Angie Smith and the newcomer came into the sheriff's office. Chap was a wrinkled, grey-haired little man, but with a mind as sharp as a Bowie knife. He assessed the stranger with a penetrating glance and decided that he looked like a man who could be trusted to do and say the right thing, but who, by doing so with the wrong person, might stir up a hornet's nest of trouble. Chap had met men like that before.

'Just in time for a fresh cup of coffee, Angie,' he said.

'Thanks, Chap, but we weren't planning on staying,' Angie said. 'Mr Leach is just dropping off Luke Trey's gun.'

Chap laughed. 'Yeah, I heard what happened in the Silver Buck.' He looked at Nat. 'Made yourself an enemy there, mister.'

'So I'm told,' Nat said. He handed over the six-gun and Chap put it in a desk drawer. He was about to turn back to the door when an afterthought occurred to him 'One thing before we go. Have you got a law dodger for someone called Jabal Hawley? Would be about ten or eleven years old – the dodger, I mean.'

Chap frowned. 'Hawley? Name seems kinda familiar. Let me take a look.' He went to a cupboard in the corner of the room and began rummaging on one of the shelves. He came out with a handful of dog-eared 'wanted' posters and lay them on the desk. He began flipping through the pile. After a minute or two he gave a sigh of satisfaction and pulled one of the dodgers free of the rest.

'This the guy you mean? It's a poor drawin'. Could be anybody.'

He turned the paper round so that Nat and Angie could see the face. It was a duplicate of the face in the newspaper cutting.

'That's him,' Nat said. 'Do me a favour, will you, Chap? Pin this up somewhere prominent. Somewhere folk'll see it as they're passing.'

'You expectin' him to arrive in town sometime soon, Mr Leach?' Chap asked

'Maybe,' Nat said. 'More likely, he's here already, but looking different.'

'That so?' Chap said, raising his eyebrows. 'Interestin'.'

'Just one other thing,' Nat added. 'Ever heard of a Travis Newton?'

There were a couple of seconds before Chap replied, 'Can't say I have.'

Nat studied him for a moment, then said, 'OK, never mind.'

It was only after Nat and Angie had left the office that Chap muttered to himself, 'Now why would he be wantin'

to know about *Travis Newton*? For reasons I know nothin'
about, nor want to know, it's a name best not mentioned
in here.'

CHAPTER 5

Nat and Angie arrived at the newspaper office at the same moment a young woman was leaving carrying a small brown-paper parcel. She was small and slim, smooth-cheeked with violet-coloured eyes, and long fair hair that hung around her shoulders. She wore a dress the colour of sunlight.

'Afternoon, Miss Brownlow,' Angie said, as they met in the doorway.

'Er . . . hello.' The young woman's face coloured as she hurried past them.

Angie shook her head, smiling. 'I reckon I embarrass her. Guess she sees me as a *fallen woman*.'

'Who is she?' Nat asked.

'Stepdaughter of Lyle Walker, one of the two men runnin' for mayor. Pretty little thing, isn't she?'

'How old is she?'

'Eighteen or nineteen. Kept her own name when her ma remarried. Not sure she's especially fond of her step pa.'

'An independent sort, then,' Nat said, approvingly.

41

They moved on inside. A young man was cleaning a flatbed printing machine while Gabe Crighton was peering at a sheet of page proofs at his desk. He was using a large magnifying glass.

'Angie!' Gabe said, looking up and smiling. 'And Mr Leach.'

'Hello Gabe, hello Toby,' Angie said.

The young man at the printing machine gave her a shy grin. 'Oh, hello Angie.'

'Don't pay no mind to Toby,' Gabe told them. 'Molly Brownlow just came in to collect some printed flyers for her step-pa's mayoral campaign, so Toby's just seen the love of his life.'

'That right, Toby?' Angie teased. 'You sweet on Miss Molly Brownlow?'

Toby laughed. 'I guess I am,' he admitted.

'And how does Miss Brownlow feel about that?' Angie asked.

'I guess she's a bit sweet on me,' Toby said. 'Trouble is, her step-pa doesn't reckon I'm good enough for her.'

'Luckily, Molly has a mind – and a will – of her own,' Gabe put in. 'Don't be fooled by that demure exterior. She's a feisty little miss when she's roused.'

'Then I wish you luck, Toby,' Angie said.

'I'll need it. I've been invited to supper this evening,' Toby said.

'My, my!' Angie said. 'You're going up in the world, Toby.' She took the newspaper cutting from her bag. 'Something I want you to look at, Gabe.'

He looked surprised, but took the cutting and immediately began reading, again using the magnifying glass.

After a minute or two he dropped it on to the desk next to the sheets of proofs. 'And you reckon this Joey kid is Joe Spearman?' he said.

'No doubt about it,' Nat said. 'I know for a fact he grew up in Stokewood, and that he worked in the livery there after his ma and pa died. He often talked about it. Never mentioned that newspaper report, though.'

'Well, it's interesting,' Gabe said. 'I suppose it might be worth a paragraph or two in the paper. Toby, come and take a look at this.'

'There's more,' Angie said. And she recounted the remarks made by Joe that morning in February.

'Hm,' Gabe said. 'That's even more interesting. Now let me guess. You want us to write an article about Joe's connection to the Stokewood killing, and the fact that he believed Jabal Hawley was still alive and well and living here in Ox Crossing.'

'And maybe hint that it might provide a motive for his killing,' Nat said.

'And what exactly do you hope to achieve by that, other than stir up a hornet's nest of speculation?'

Nat shrugged. 'Who can say? At the very least, maybe Jabal Hawley – or whatever he's calling himself now – will start to feel a mite uncomfortable.'

'Or maybe your friend got it wrong. Looking at that picture in the report, I can't say it reminds me of anybody in particular,' Gabe said.

'In which case I'll have to start looking for another reason why somebody should've felt the need to stick a knife in him,' Nat said. 'Joe was a good friend of mine. I don't aim to let his killer go unpunished.'

'Will you do it, Gabe?' Angie asked.

Gabe turned to his young assistant. 'What do you reckon, Toby?' He looked back at Angie and Nat. 'Toby does most of the writing these days. My eyesight isn't what it was. He's pretty damn good at it, too. When I'm gone to meet my maker, which could be any time soon when you get to my age, Toby'll be running the whole show here.'

'It could make an interesting article,' Toby said, scanning the newspaper report and looking up. 'Guess I could pull something together.'

Gabe nodded. 'You're right. OK, Mr Leach. We'll do what you ask, and we'll see what happens.'

'Thanks,' Nat said. 'By the way, the name's Nat.'

Sheriff Chesney Francome was dismounting his horse outside his office after the ride back from the Circle C when he saw Angie Smith and the nosy newcomer to town – the one enquiring about Travis Newton – emerge from the newspaper office.

'Now just what have those two been doin'?' he muttered under his breath. The mere sight of the stranger set Francome's nerves on edge. Cleve Connor's assurances that he'd 'deal with' the man if he looked like being trouble had failed to set Francome's mind at rest.

Not that his ride back from the Circle C had done anything to lighten his mood. Something Cleve had said had gnawed at his conscience the whole way back. *One of these days you'll use it in front of somebody who gets curious.* The 'it' he had been referring to was Cleve's real name, of course. Trouble was, Francome had already done that. It had just slipped out when he'd had a few too many drinks at a social occasion. Now he just had to hope that the person he'd told had forgotten all about it.

Because if Cleve ever found out . . .

He felt the urgent need of a strong drink, but when he saw that Angie and her companion were heading towards the Silver Buck, he decided to resort to the bottle of red eye he kept in his office, rather than patronize the saloon. He had no wish to meet up with the inquisitive *hombre* until he'd found out more about him. To do this, he resolved to ask a few questions of Gabe Crighton, seeing as the newspaper office had been the couple's last port of call.

But only after he'd had a drink.

His deputy was sitting in the battered armchair next to the window, reading a dime novel and drinking a cup of coffee. Chap Fancy had a liking for these lurid stories, the more sensational the better. He also drank enough coffee to float a ship.

'Busy, Chap?' Francome snapped, slamming the door behind him. 'Don't let me interrupt anythin' important.'

Chap looked up from his book. 'Kinda tetchy, ain't we?' He saw Francome head for the drawer where he kept the bottle of red eye. 'Tetchy an' in need of a drink. Now who's been yankin' your tail?'

Francome poured himself a shot of whiskey and downed it in one gulp. After a moment, he poured himself another. 'Just seen Angie Smith an' that newcomer comin' from the newspaper office,' he said.

'They were here earlier,' Chap told him.

Francome choked on his drink. 'Th-they were?' he spluttered. 'What'n hell for?'

45

'The man's name is Leach, an' he had an argument with Luke Trey,' Chap informed him. 'Took Trey's gun away from him an' told him he could collect it here later today. Leach an' Angie were droppin' it off. It's in the desk drawer if Trey should come for it when I ain't here.'

'That all they wanted?'

'Nope. They had me dig out an old law dodger for a fellah called Hawley. Jabal Hawley. He's wanted for a killin' in Stokewood, some eleven years ago. Leach asked me to put it up somewhere prominent so folks would see it.' He pointed to the office window. 'So I stuck it there, facin' out.'

'What's his interest in Hawley?' Francome asked.

Chap shrugged. 'He didn't say.'

Francome's first thought was to take the dodger down. They weren't here to pander to Leach. Who the hell did he think he was? Then again, he wanted to avoid a confrontation with the man who was also asking about Travis Newton.

'Guess it won't do any harm,' he said.

'Wanted to know if'n I'd heard of a Travis Newton,' Chap said, casually. ' 'Course I told him no, I hadn't, an' – you all right Ches? You've gone kinda pale?'

'Yeah, I'm all right!' Francome snapped.

'You ever heard of a Travis. . . ?'

'*No*! Go back to your book!' He put the bottle of red eye back in the drawer. 'I'm goin' to see Gabe Crighton.'

'What happened to you?' Cleve Connor asked. He was standing by the corral watching one of his men examining one of the horses. The animal appeared lame for some reason. His question was addressed to Luke Trey, who had just arrived back at the Circle C, his right hand bandaged.

'Some bastard got the drop on me,' Trey replied. 'Took my god-damned gun away, too.'

'I noticed the empty holster,' Connor said, nodding towards Trey's gunbelt. 'He still have it?'

Trey shook his head. 'Told me I could collect it from Francome's office. Damn it! He expects me to go crawlin' to our piss-poor sheriff just to get my six-shooter back.'

'Don't worry about that,' Connor said. 'I'll send one of the men to collect it. Anyway, I'm sure you've got another.'

'Too right,' Trey said, forcefully.

'So who was the *hombre* you got into a tangle with?'

'Stranger called Leach. I got his name from the hotel clerk. Bastard's a walkin' corpse, though. Nobody gets the drop on Luke Trey an' gets away with it.'

'Leave him be for the time being,' Connor told him. 'I want to find out a little more about Mr Leach.'

Trey frowned. 'Why, boss?'

'I've got my reasons,' Connor said. 'I'll let you know when you can take him on again. Although if he's as fast as you're implying, maybe you should take him by surprise.' He looked directly at the other man. 'The way you bushwhacked the Spearman fellah.'

Trey looked startled. 'How did you know-?'

Connor scowled at him. 'I didn't. At least, I wasn't sure – until now. I don't mind you doing a bit of freelancing, but you work for me, Luke, remember that.'

'Yeah, sure, boss. You'll always come first.'

'How much did he pay you to kill Spearman, this person? No, don't tell me his name, I don't want to know, although I think I can guess.'

'Fifty bucks,' Trey said.

'Hell, Luke, you come cheap. Next time ask him for double. Why did he want Spearman killed?'

'He didn't say, an' I didn't ask.'

'Probably best,' Connor agreed. He looked thoughtful. 'Be interesting to find out, though.'

CHAPTER 6

'I know your first priority now is to find your army buddy's killer, Nat,' Angie said, 'but are you going to tell me about this Travis Newton you're so keen to find?'

They were back in Angie's office, having decided to give the saloon a miss. What they were about to discuss required privacy.

A pot of coffee stood on the desk between them. Angie sat in her swivel chair whilst Nat sprawled in an easy chair with a faded floral pattern on its covers. He was nursing a mug of black coffee.

'Must be important,' Angie persisted, sensing Nat's reluctance but determined to satisfy her curiosity.

'Yeah, it's important,' Nat said, taking a swig from his mug.

'So, who is he?'

Nat sighed. 'Newton's one of four confederate deserters who raped and killed my mother and sister,' he said, the words coming out in a sudden rush. 'Something I discovered when I went home after the War. My pa died at

Gettysburg so, thank God, he never found out what happened to them.'

'Jeeze!' Angie reached across the desk and put a hand over his. 'Nat, I'm so sorry.'

'Of the four men, two are dead,' Nat continued. 'One was shot for desertion, when he was caught. The other died in Yuma prison where he was serving time for killing a man in a card game. His name was Brooks. Took me four years to track him down. When I did, he was already dying of cancer, but he told me the names of two of his compatriots – Cyrus Cutler and Travis Newton. Cutler was the one the army caught and shot for desertion, so I didn't have to go looking for him. He was also Brooks' cousin. Travis Newton, as far as Brooks knew, was still alive but he didn't know where.'

'And the fourth man?' Angie prompted, when Nat paused.

'That's what's odd. Brooks knew his name all right, but he wouldn't tell me it, and nothing I could say would make him. Fact he seemed afraid to, almost as if he thought by telling me he'd be signing my death warrant.'

'Strange,' Angie said.

'I got the feeling Brooks was relieved, after all these years, to confess to his part in the murders,' Nat went on. 'He kept saying how sorry he was, and how he'd just been caught up in the moment, and how he wished there was something he could do to put it right. 'Course there wasn't, 'cepting give me the names of the others. But when it came to the fourth man, it was as though he was protecting me by not revealing it.'

'Sounds like he's real dangerous to know, this mystery

50

man,' Angie said.

'Makes no never-mind,' Nat said. 'I'll track him down eventually.'

'Then what? What are you planning to do to him and this Newton man?'

A faraway look came into Nat's eyes. 'I'll kill them,' he said simply.

They were quiet for several minutes. Then Angie said, 'How did you track down Brooks?'

'Sheer chance,' Nat said. 'I was working as shotgun rider for a stage line in Kansas. On long journeys you and the driver get to know one another pretty well, get to talking about family and where you come from and things.'

'Natural thing to do,' Angie said. 'You told him about your wife and sister?'

Nat nodded. 'And this is where luck, chance, fate – call it what you like – stepped in. It turned out he had been in jail with Cyrus Cutler while Cutler was waiting to be executed. The two men shared a cell. The driver – Bernie Ludgate, his name was – was serving a three-month sentence for stealing chickens.' Nat chuckled. 'Imagine it. A murderer-rapist sharing a cell with a chicken thief! Anyways, it seems Cutler talked a lot in his sleep, and the name Eli Brooks kept coming up. Bernie asked him who this Eli Brooks fellah was that seemed to haunt Cutler's bad dreams. Well Cutler, knowing he was going to die in a matter of days, admitted Eli was his cousin and that they had done something bad. Something much worse than deserting the army. Something he bitterly regretted. After a lot of persuasion on Bernie's part – he always was a curious cuss, was Bernie – Cutler told his story. But he refused to name the other two men involved in the killings. Said it was best if Bernie didn't know, implying it would be bad for Bernie's health!

'But now I had a name to work on. Even so, it was another year before I got my next lead. I was working as a deputy marshal in a small town thirty miles north of Yuma. I'd only had the job a couple of weeks when I was looking through some old law dodgers and came across the name: Eli Brooks. Wanted for murder. Well, I started to ask the marshal about him, but he cut me off. "That's an old dodger," he said. "The guy's in Yuma prison, so you can throw it away." 'Course I didn't, I folded it up and put it in my pocket. First chance I got, I paid Brooks a visit in Yuma and got his version of the story, and the name Travis Newton.'

'And Newton's connection with Ox Crossing?' Angie queried.

'It's the place Newton mentioned when Brooks last saw him. Newton paid him a visit in Yuma, a few months before I saw him. Seems Newton was a close cohort with the fourth man – the mystery man – and had been sent to make sure Brooks had kept his mouth shut. Newton's job was to verify this and warn Brooks to continue to keep his mouth shut. 'Course, Newton didn't know Brooks was dying.'

'Or that you, the son and brother of the women they'd killed, was about to pay Brooks a visit,' Angie put in.

' 'Xactly,' Nat agreed. 'And dying is a pretty good incentive for unburdening your soul.'

'So if Newton was, or is, a cohort of the fourth man,

maybe the two of them are here in Ox Crossing,' Angie said.

'Seems likely,' Nat said. 'Only they've changed their names, Brooks told me, although he didn't know to what. But if I can find Newton, I'm sure I can persuade him to name the fourth man.'

Angie smiled. 'I'm sure you can.'

CHAPTER 7

Lyle Walker watched approvingly as his step-daughter approached the house. He was sitting by the window of the room that overlooked a large stretch of lawn and shrubs, neatly divided by a winding path leading to the front door of the building. The large frame house was gothic in Style, but not ostentatious. Strictly speaking it was not Lyle's house. His wife, Jane Brownlow as she had been before she'd married Lyle, had lived here with her husband and had inherited it on his death. And her marriage to Lyle Walker had not changed that.

It was an arrangement that was perfectly agreeable to Lyle. After all, he had acquired a dozen or more properties and businesses in the town in the five years since he had arrived in Ox Crossing. And he would be the first to admit that his success was due in a large part to Jane's popularity with the townsfolk, and, to begin with, not a little of Jane's money. Henry Brownlow had himself been a successful land and property speculator when alive; naturally the bulk of his estate had gone to his wife, with some money left in trust for his daughter when she came of age.

Molly had been just twelve when her father had died.

Lyle had got a job as a clerk in the bank soon after he arrived in Ox Crossing. He had proved to be good with figures, and was well liked by customers. Jane Brownlow had an account at the bank, and began paying what seemed to be rather more visits than were necessary for everyday business. In truth there was an almost instant attraction between the two of them, and after a respectable amount of time, they had begun attending church and various town functions as a couple. Marriage was the next logical step.

Jane's popularity was something that Lyle continued to capitalize on, and which he hoped would win him the position of mayor in the forthcoming contest.

Now as he smoked a cheroot, stroked his walrus moustache and contemplated Molly's approach up the path, he counted her as another aspect of his good fortune. Even so, he had to admit relations between them had cooled somewhat since Lyle had voiced his disapproval of Molly's liking for young Toby Greenway at the newspaper office. Also Jane seemed happy to give her blessing to the friendship, which didn't help. She had even invited the kid to supper that evening, Lyle remembered. So perhaps it was time to set aside his objections and restore a measure of harmony between himself and his step-daughter.

Besides, there were more important things to be thinking about if he hoped to defeat Howard Ellis in the mayoral election. In many ways, what it came down to was which man managed to get the backing of Cleve Connor, but Connor had up to now been tantalisingly cagey about where his vote would go. One thing was certain, when he did finally announce his support for one of the candidates, a good many people would follow suit. They would be too afraid not to.

And so far Howard Ellis seemed to be the favourite.

But there was time for that to change. Not least because Lyle knew something Cleve Connor would want to keep quiet. And sometimes a man's silence had to be bought.

Chesney Francome walked up the street to the newspaper office, constantly looking around, not wanting to come face to face with the Leach character. When the two men did finally meet, Francome wanted it to be on his terms. Secretly, he hoped Cleve would take it into his head to have Luke Trey put a bullet in the nosy critter.

One thing puzzled Francome. Why was Leach interested in a killing that happened years ago in Stokewood, a town a hundred or more miles away, and by somebody Francome had never heard of. Maybe Gabe Crighton would be able to enlighten him.

The newspaperman was alone in his office, having just finished printing that week's edition of *The Weekly Crossing*, ready for distribution the next day. He was enjoying a quiet smoke and a glass of whiskey when Francome came in the door.

'Where's your sidekick?' Francome asked.

'I let him off early,' Gabe said, with a twinkle in his eye. 'He's got an important date so he needs time to spruce himself up.'

Francome wasn't interested in Toby Greenway's social life, but he was pleased to have the opportunity to speak with Gabe in private.

'You had visitors earlier,' he said.

'I did?' Gabe adopted a cagey tone.

'Yeah, I saw them leavin'. Angie Smith an' that Leach guy.'

'Oh, them.'

'Yeah, them. What did they want?'

'Now that's newspaper business, Ches,' Gabe said. 'Although you'll find out soon enough from an article in tomorrow's paper.'

'What's it about, this *article*?' Francome was suddenly nervous.

'You'll just have to wait until tomorrow and see,' Gabe told him.

'Dammit, Gabe, why the secrecy?'

'People tell me things in confidence,' Gabe said. He knew he was being obstructive, but he wanted to see just how desperate the sheriff was and what exactly he was after. For, remembering the newspaper cutting he had tucked away in his desk drawer, it had occurred to Gabe in the last few moments that Chesney Francome was roughly the age Jabal Hawley would be now.

But Francome's next question seemed to allay his suspicions and raise others.

'Did Leach ask about anybody called Travis Newton? Is that what your article's goin' to be about?'

Francome tried to sound casual, but it didn't fool Gabe.

'Well, he did mention that name, it's true.'

'Did he say why he was interested?'

'Not to me,' Gabe said. *But I wouldn't mind betting Angie's got it out of him by now* was his unspoken thought. 'Do you know something about this Newton character?'

'No,' Francome said quickly. Too quickly, Gabe thought.

'Maybe we'll tag the name on to the end of the article, or mention it somewhere else in the paper,' Gabe said, taunting the lawman. ' "Does anybody know the where-abouts of the mysterious Travis Newton?" Something like that. Yes, it might make a paragraph or two.'

'Now listen here, Gabe,' Francome said, an angry tremor in his voice. 'Keep the name out of your god-damned paper. An' if anyone mentions it to you, come an' tell me.'

'Really, Ches? It's that important? Who is the guy, do you *know* him? Is he some sort of gunslinger?' Gabe was getting the feeling he had a tiger by the tail and he was extra curious to learn the reason. There was little doubt in his mind that the sheriff *did* know the man in question, or at least knew something about him.

Francome seemed about to say more, then changed his mind. 'Forget it,' he said, visibly trying to steady himself. 'Just don't go writin' anythin' about him.'

And with that, Francome stormed out of the newspaper office.

After he had gone, Gabe took up a copy of the newspa-per and re-read the article Toby had written earlier that day. It seemed to cover all the points Nat Leach wanted mentioned. But was there more to find out? Maybe Joe Spearing had only kept the particular cutting in which he featured. Was there a follow-up report giving more details of the crime?

Gabe knew the editor of the *Stokewood Gazette* – Bud Weston. They had once worked on the same newspaper and had met once or twice over the years. And occasionally they fed one another bits of information or gossip if they thought it might be useful to one or the other of them.

'Maybe I'll send him a wire,' he said to himself. He checked his fob watch. 'Telegraph office should still be open.'

Cliff Jarvis, telegraph operator and compulsive gossip, watched Gabe Crighton leave the telegraph office. Ten minutes later, he put a 'Back Soon' notice on the door, shut the office, and headed off along the street. He had scribbled a copy of the wire the newspaper editor had sent to his counterpart in Stokewood on a piece of paper. This he would give to the person who, some long time ago, had paid him handsomely to tip off the contents of any wire sent by any person which referred to the town of Stokewood. This person had not enlightened Cliff as to the reason for wanting the information, but had sworn Cliff to secrecy with a promise of a bonus if ever such a wire was sent, and a further payment for a copy of any reply to the wire.

Several years had passed and Cliff had almost forgotten about the agreement. Then the name of the town had cropped up in Gabe Crighton's wire. And now, to his secret delight, Cliff was about to collect the first part of his bonus.

CHAPTER 8

Toby Greenway was feeling uncomfortably full. Maybe he shouldn't have had that second helping of apple pie that Mrs Walker had urged upon him. Or the large glass of wine. Toby wasn't used to wine and, to be truthful, it had given him a bit of a headache. All of which was unfortunate, as here he was, sitting on the back veranda on a starlit night sharing the swing seat with the love of his life.

'Everything all right, Toby?' Molly asked.

She was looking particularly lovely tonight, he decided, in that purple velvet dress with the lace trimmings, her hair shining in the moonlight.

'Everything's fine,' Toby replied. He placed a hand over hers. 'You're so beautiful, Molly. Your pa's probably right, I don't deserve you.'

'Actually, I think my *step*-pa's warming to you,' she said. 'Not that I care.' She leaned across and kissed him lightly on the lips.

'But it's all pretty hopeless, you know that, don't you?' he said. 'Me, working for a weekly newsrag. You, daughter of one of Ox Crossing's richest residents. A man about to be mayor, maybe.'

'It'll work out,' Molly said. 'And one of these days it will be *your* newspaper. Mr Crighton told me so, ages ago.'

'Even so, I'll never be rich enough to satisfy your stepfather.'

'Don't worry about it. Ma's on our side,' Molly said.

'She is?'

Molly nodded. 'And she'll work on my stepfather and bring him round.'

Toby looked at her. 'You never call him "Pa", do you?'

Her look hardened. 'He isn't my pa. Oh, he's kind enough to me. He'd spoil me if I let him, but I don't. Anyway, let's change the subject.'

'OK,' Toby said.

'I passed that Smith woman when I was coming out of the newspaper office. She was with a man I didn't recognize.' Molly shuddered. 'She always speaks to me, and I never know where to put myself when I think of what she . . . well, *does*.'

Toby laughed. 'Angie's all right, and . . .'

'*Angie*! Toby Greenway, are you saying you know her well enough to call her by her first name? Well, I never. . . !'

Toby put a hand across her lips. 'Shh! No, of course I don't know her *that* well, if you mean what I think you mean. It's just that she's a friend of Gabe's, and sometimes drops by for a chat and a cup of coffee. And the first time I called her Miss Smith she told me not to be so formal and would I please call her Angie. As a matter of fact she's a nice lady.'

'*Lady*?'

'Well, woman then,' Toby acknowledged.

'Who was the man she was with? One of her . . . clients?'

'No, at least I don't think so. He was a friend of that young guy who got shot a few months back. Joe Spearing. Matter of fact, they came with an interesting story. I wrote an article for this week's edition. You'll be able to read it tomorrow. Gabe thought I made a pretty good job of it.'

Molly tucked an arm through his and put her head on his shoulder. 'See? One day you'll be a famous writer, and then even Mr Lyle Walker will have to sit up and take note.'

Toby kissed the top of her head. 'I'll settle for being a good newspaperman,' he said. 'And, if I'm lucky, your husband.'

Molly turned and looked up at him. 'You won't need luck for that,' she said. And pressed her lips against his.

CHAPTER 9

At ten o'clock the following morning, copies of *The Weekly Crossing* hit the streets and Toby's article, carefully edited by Gabe to make sure they were not breaking any defamation laws, was given front page prominence.

The reply to Gabe's wire to Bud Weston came an hour later, too late to add anything to the article. Not that it mattered, as Gabe never got it.

Cliff Jarvis, on reading the wire just minutes after reading Toby Greenway's newspaper article, sat and thought for a considerable while. Even though the wire's contents made little sense to him, the more he thought about them, the more certain he became that what he was holding could prove more valuable than he'd first thought. And to the person concerned, might be more explosive than a stick of dynamite.

One thing he was confident about. They offered an opportunity to extract a much bigger payment than the second half of his expected bonus.

Didn't they?

There was only one way to find out.

Once again, he put the 'Back Soon' notice on the tele-graph office door and, with the wire in his pocket, set off.

Late that evening, an exhausted Cliff Jarvis rolled off the perky little redhead whose name was Rosalie. She was one of Angie Smith's 'girls'.

'Was that nice, sugar?' Rosalie enquired. She always asked, more out of habit than concern. Cliff, whose pink and portly body reminded her of pictures she had seen of a beached jellyfish, had barely managed to perform, the result of too much whiskey in the Silver Buck. It had taken a good deal of Rosalie's skill to 'raise an interest', so to speak, and get him started.

She watched as he sat on the side of the bed and strug-gled into his check suit pants. As he got to his feet, a leather wallet fell from the back pocket. Cliff didn't notice it, but Rosalie picked it up from the floor. And her eyes opened wide when she saw that it was stuffed with paper money.

'Jeeze, Cliff,' she said. 'Did you rob a bank before you came to visit me? There must be best part of a thousand dollars here.'

Cliff snatched it from her grasp. 'Give it here!'

'OK, take it easy, lover,' Rosalie said. 'I'm no thief.'

Cliff calmed down after a moment and grinned. 'Nope, didn' rob a bank,' he said, slurring his words and tucking his shirt into his pants. 'Didn' need to. Fellah who gave it me was buyin' my silence, see? Payin' me to be *discreet*.' He swayed on his feet and slumped into the chair next to the bed. After two attempts to put his shoes on, Rosalie got down on her knees to lend a hand.

'And who was this fellah?' she asked, casually.

Cliff tapped the side of his nose. 'That'd be tellin'. 'Sides, I've got the feelin' he might be willin' to *keep* payin' for my discretion, now that I know somethin' he wouldn't want spread around.' He put on his jacket and patted one of the pockets. 'I'm smart, y'see. I've still got the wire – well, best you don't know, sweetie, then you can't tell nobody.'

He pulled a couple of bills from the wallet and stuffed them in Rosalie's cleavage before staggering out into the night.

Luke Trey watched him emerge from the whorehouse and head towards the saloon. After checking that nobody was paying a particular interest in what was happening, Luke crossed the street in four fast paces and grabbed the other man's arm.

'Gotta talk to you, Cliff,' he said, steering him towards the same alleyway where Joe Spearing's body had been discovered.

'Wh. . .!' Cliff began. 'Hey, you're hurtin' me!'

The alleyway was dark, other than for a shaft of moonlight at one end. Luke pushed him into the shadows, then took his .45 from his belt and shoved the barrel up under Cliff's chin.

'Give!' he said, opening the palm of his free hand.

'Wh-what?' Cliff asked.

'The wire, an' what's left of the money.'

For a second or two, Cliff looked about to argue but changed his mind quickly as the pressure of metal against his neck increased. With a shaking hand, he took the wallet from his pants. Before he had a chance to extract the bills, Luke had snatched it from him and stuffed it into his shirt pocket.

'Now the wire,' Luke demanded.

'How d'you know. . . ?' Cliff began.

'*Give!*'

Cliff choked as the gun bit into his flesh. 'Coat . . . pocket!' he managed to gasp.

Luke shoved a hand in the jacket pocket and retrieved the telegraph.

'Wh.. what're you gonna do now?' Cliff said, his voice a hoarse whisper.

Luke Trey smiled.

And pulled the trigger.

Cliff's body was found some minutes later, the gunshot having roused Ted Brewster from the saddle shop. Ted had been working on his books before heading off to bed, and since the alleyway was next door to his shop, he couldn't help but hear the shot. But by the time he got outside and round to the alleyway, the killer had vanished – almost certainly by way of the opening at the far end, which led into a maze of backstreets. Ted ran to alert the sheriff.

Word of the killing spread quickly, and there was soon a small gathering of people, including Gabe Crighton and Jasper Harrison, the town's undertaker.

'It's as though you've got a second sense when it comes to dead bodies, Jasper,' Gabe said. 'Can you *smell* potential business?'

Jasper laughed. 'Hello, Gabe. How are you?'

'Not ready for you just yet, my friend.'

Gabe turned to the sheriff, who was staring at Cliff Jarvis' body and wringing his hands.

'Why would anybody kill Jarvis?' Gabe said.

'How in hell should I know?' Francome snapped.

'Well, I reckon you should try to find out pronto,' Gabe said. 'Two killings are liable to make folks nervous. First Joe Spearing gets bushwhacked, now Jarvis. And in the same alleyway. What's going on?'

'Don't mean to say the two are connected,' Francome said. 'One was a knifin', the other a shootin'.'

'Bit of a coincidence if they aren't,' Gabe said. 'Ox Crossing's a quiet sort of town normally. How many killings have there been here in the last five years, other than those caused by an argument and a shoot-out? Just these two, that's all. Got to be a connection.'

'OK, OK!' Francome shouted. 'I'll look into it!'

And you'll look about as far as you did for the Spearing killing, no further than the end of your nose, unless Cleve Connor tells you to.

Gabe's thoughts went unexpressed.

CHAPTER 10

Next morning, Gabe was finishing breakfast at Freda's when Nat found him.

'Howdy,' Gabe said. 'Coffee?'

'Sure.' Nat sat down opposite him.

Gabe waved Freda across and she came clutching the coffee pot.

'You want breakfast, Mr Leach?' she asked.

'No, I'm OK, Freda.' He waited until she had retreated to the kitchen before addressing Gabe. 'So what do you reckon to the latest killing? Connected to the newspaper report about Stokewood and Jabal Hawley?'

'Be an odd coincidence if it wasn't,' Gabe said. 'But there's more.'

'There is?'

Gabe nodded. 'Four days ago I sent a wire to an old friend of mine, Bud Weston. He's editor of the *Stokewood Gazette*. I asked him if there was any more he could add to the newspaper report Joe Spearing had kept all these years. I thought maybe there'd been a follow-up with some fresh information about the fire and the killing. Maybe

68

background on Jabal Hawley, or even the man who'd been shot.'

'Martin Benson,' Nat said.

'Right,' Gabe said.

'What did Weston have to tell you? Anything?'

'Well, that's just it. I've not received a reply.'

'Maybe he had nothing further to tell,' Nat said.

'Then Bud would have sent a reply saying so, I know he would.'

'So what are you suggesting?'

'That maybe there *was* an answer to my wire, but for some reason, Cliff Jarvis decided not to tell me.' Gabe paused, then said, 'And now he's dead.'

Nat swallowed a mouthful of coffee, considering the implications. 'You said "for some reason". What reason could Jarvis have had? You knew him, was he some sort of *opportunist?*'

'Well, for starters, he was a gossip. Folks were never sure their wires remained confidential, the way they were supposed to.'

'And you think he might have blabbed and by doing so put himself in danger?'

Gabe shook his head. 'If that had been the case, he would have given me Bud's wire before spreading the word about its contents. No, I think you're right. I think it more likely that whatever Bud Weston had to tell me, as soon as Jarvis read it he saw it as a means to make money.'

'Blackmail,' Nat said.

'Exactly.'

'Which implies that something in Bud Weston's wire gave a clue, or even a clear pointer, to the present identity of Jabal Hawley.'

'That's what I reckon,' Gabe said. 'And when Jarvis tried to use the information to extract money from Hawley, he signed his own death warrant. Remember, Hawley killed Joe Spearing when he felt his past was threatening to catch up with him.'

'I don't believe Joe would have tried to blackmail Hawley,' Nat said. 'But he might have been planning to go to the law and expose him, and then collect the $1,000 reward.'

'But he was murdered before he got the chance. Which means Hawley must have got wind of Joe's suspicions when Joe started asking questions.'

'None of this gets us any further in finding Hawley.'

'But another wire to my friend asking him to repeat what he said in his first reply just might,' Gabe said. 'Which is why I plan to head for the telegraph office when I leave here.'

'Meantime, we need to keep looking,' Nat said. 'It's just possible Hawley – or whoever he is now – will get spooked and clear out of town.'

'At least then we'll know who Hawley is,' Gabe said. 'But let's remember what Angie said about the morning Joe looked out of her bedroom window. Only four of the men in the street fitted the bill as far as age and general appearance went: Cleve Connor, Otis Bream, Howard Ellis and Ches Francome. Of the other two she spotted, Lyle Walker would be too old and Luke Trey too young.'

'So we need to know when the four came here and where they came from,' Nat said.

'They all arrived after the end of the War, at various

times,' Gabe said. 'Connor and Francome arrived together, about three years ago. Where from is anybody's guess. They've never said, and they've always sidestepped the question. Connor bought the Circle C, and for a time, Francome worked for him. Then Connor persuaded townsfolk to elect Francome as sheriff after the last holder of that post left town kinda suddenly.'

'Left town?' Nat said, frowning.

'I know what you're thinking,' Gabe said. 'And it *was* a bit of a mystery. One day he was here, the next day he was gone. We've never seen him since, nor heard where he went.'

'So his disappearance could be down to Connor,' Nat said. 'As a way of getting the sheriff he wanted.'

Gabe nodded. 'That's what a lot of folk suspected. Proving it was another matter.'

'What about Bream and Ellis?'

'Howard Ellis arrived a few months after the war. Set up his practice as the town's one and only lawyer, and pretty soon got himself elected as mayor, a post he's held since then.'

'Where did he come from?'

' "A little town in Wyoming you'll never have heard of", was what he told us.'

'Hang on,' Nat said. 'Stokewood's in Wyoming, isn't it?'

'It is, and it hasn't escaped my notice,' Gabe said.

'Then we should ask him to be more specific.'

Gabe shook his head. 'Wouldn't help. Even if he did come from Stokewood, he's not going to tell us, is he? He'll just name another small town in that state.'

'I guess you're right.'

'Although I think it's stretching it a bit to think a small-time farmer – which is what Jabal Hawley was – would be intelligent enough to study and qualify as a lawyer, even in eleven years.'

'Which leaves Bream.'

'Otis is a better prospect. He has his own farm ten miles north of town. He arrived a year after the War ended with enough money to set himself up. Said he had a farm in New Mexico before the war, though of course that could be a lie if he's Jabal Hawley. Apparently his wife died from consumption, again before the war, which is why he wanted a fresh start somewhere else.'

'None of this helps us much then,' Nat said. 'Although Cleve Connor sounds more of a killer than the other three.'

Gabe fiddled with his coffee cup and looked away. 'Connor . . . yes.'

'Something on your mind?' Nat asked.

'Look, don't get mad, but Angie told me why you came to Ox Crossing and why you're looking for a man called Travis Newton,' Gabe admitted. 'Truth is, she was busting to tell somebody something and I . . . well. . . .'

'You got it out of her,' Nat finished for him.

'It'll go no further,' Gabe assured him. 'But there's something more. Sheriff Francome was asking me about the name Travis Newton, after he heard you were looking for the man. He quickly denied all knowledge of him himself when I asked him. Too quickly, it seemed to me. Then he got real jumpy when I suggested I might mention the name in the paper.'

'Did he now? That's interesting,' Nat said. 'Think I

might pay him a visit.'

'Thought you might,' Gabe said. 'But be careful. If Connor is Travis Newton, you could be risking a bullet in the back.' He got up from the table. 'Anyway, I'm off to the telegraph office to see Nora Millington. She's the new telegraph officer, I gather from Freda. Let's hope she's a bit more discreet than Cliff Jarvis ever was. And less opportunistic.'

Luke Trey, richer by a hundred dollars than he'd been twenty-four hours earlier, sat sprawled in a chair at one of the tables in the Silver Buck. It was still early in the day, but a bottle of red eye and a shot glass stood on the table in front of him.

He had already dismissed all thoughts of the previous night's shooting. Cliff Jarvis had meant nothing to him, other than the object of a useful payoff. He had returned both the wire and what was left of the money in Jarvis' wallet to the man who had commissioned his services. He had been tempted to remove some of the cash in the wallet for himself, but had resisted for some reason he couldn't have explained. As to the contents of the wire, he had tried to read them, but, with his poor reading skills, they had made little sense to him. But then, Luke never tried to read *The Weekly Crossing* so had no knowledge of the eleven-year-old Stokewood crime and its possible links to the man who had paid him his hundred dollars.

So he was feeling pleasantly satisfied with himself when Chesney Francome came into the saloon. The sheriff looked round the room, spotted Luke and made a beeline for him. The latter's feelings of contentment dissipated the closer the lawman got to his table. He had a good idea what was coming.

Francome pulled out the chair opposite Luke and sank into it.

'I guess I can put down last night's killin' to you, Trey.'

Luke made no reply. Instead he signalled to the barkeep to bring another glass. When this had been done, he poured a shot of whiskey and pushed it across to Francome.

'Guessin's all you're gonna be able to do, sheriff,' Luke said. 'Got no witnesses, have you?'

'I've got a lotta people puttin' pressure on me to do somethin', is what I've got,' Francome said. He swallowed the shot of red eye and poured himself another. 'On whose orders were you actin'? Cleve's? Can't think why Cleve should want a nobody like Jarvis out of the way. Now if it had been the Leach guy. . . .'

Luke's face darkened at the mention of the man who'd taken his gun away from him. 'Don't worry, Leach is a walkin' dead man once Cleve gives the word. Told me to hold off for the time bein', but I'm gettin' kinda impatient.'

'So who did tell you to kill Jarvis?'

'Who said I did kill him? Could've been anybody. From what I've heard he was a nosy sonofabitch. Sorta guy askin' to get a bullet in his head.'

Francome sighed. He could see he was getting nowhere. He downed his drink and got to his feet. 'Reckon I'll go an' see Cleve. Maybe get him to give you the nod to get rid of Leach.'

'Suits me,' Luke said. 'Sooner the better.'

74

*

Gabe, having sent a fresh wire to Bud Weston in Stokewood, made his way to the newspaper office. Toby was already there, looking at some notes he'd made on the murder of Cliff Jarvis.

'I'm real sorry for Mr Jarvis,' Toby said, 'but at least it's another proper newspaper story to write up. Until a little while ago it was all beef prices and the church socials for copy.'

'Beef prices and church socials will do fine for me.' Gabe said. 'Last thing we need in Ox Crossing is a mystery killer.'

'Most people seem to think it was Luke Trey, acting on Cleve Connor's orders,' Toby said.

'And why would Connor want Cliff Jarvis dead?' Gabe queried. He decided to keep his thoughts about the missing wire to himself for the time being.

'It would have to be something to do with a wire Connor sent or received,' Toby said. 'Everybody knows Cliff read people's wires and was a blabbermouth. Maybe a wire came for Connor that had some information that Connor didn't want spread around, and he shut Cliff up before he had the chance to say anything. Shut him up permanently.'

You could be right, son, only the 'information' might have had more to do with the Stokewood fire and murder. Gabe kept his suspicions to himself. He would await Bud Weston's wire before taking Toby into his confidence. For one thing, whatever it was Bud had said in his first wire had seemingly got a man killed. So his second wire might be equally dangerous, and Gabe had no intention of putting Toby in harm's way. It was all right for him, he was an old man, but Toby had his whole life ahead of him.

CHAPTER 11

When Nat left Freda's café, he went to the livery to check on his horse. He wanted to make sure the liveryman was earning his fee. Nat and the chestnut gelding had been together since the War and there was a mutual affection between them.

His visit to the livery turned out to be fortuitous, because whilst he was talking with the liveryman he saw Sheriff Francome heading out of town.

'Guess I'll stretch my animal's legs for a spell,' Nat said. 'Where's my saddle?'

Ten minutes later he was trailing the lawman through a canyon as black clouds hung overhead and the first splats of rain sent up puffs of dust from the parched trail. A jagged streak of lightning was followed seconds later by a clap of thunder. It echoed through the canyon and Nat cursed his lack of a slicker as a sudden downpour swept across the landscape.

The gelding's hoofs splashed through puddles and Nat pulled his Stetson low over his face to keep the rain out of his eyes. As far as he could remember, Francome had also been without a slicker so at least they were in the same boat.

It soon became clear the sheriff was headed for the Circle C ranch, but it took a further half hour before the rain eased and Nat came to a rocky crest and looked down into the valley. From there he could make out the sprawling stone-built Circle C ranch house and its outbuildings. He could also see the figure of Francome dismounting outside the porch.

Seeing three men working in the corral and conscious that if he could see them they would be able to see him, Nat looked around for cover. Whilst his first instinct was to follow Francome and himself pay a visit to Cleve Connor, he decided to consider his options before taking any action. Seeing a drift of pine trees a short distance to his right, he gigged the chestnut gelding towards them.

Nat assumed he was unobserved.

He was wrong.

Luke Trey had taken a different route to the Circle C, using an old stagecoach trail. But as he neared his destination, he spotted the rider on the ridge overlooking the ranch. And it took him less than a minute to put a name to him.

'Leach!' he muttered to himself, then cursed.

He debated what to do, and as Nat moved off into the trees, decided to bide his time and await events. Even though he was itching to put a bullet in the bastard, Cleve hadn't given the go-ahead to kill him, and probably had his reasons for delaying.

Luke also recognized Francome's mount outside the

ranch house and had no desire to meet up with the lawman yet again. He moved his horse into a position where he could watch things happening unseen, and pulled out the makings of a smoke.

'I'm tellin' you, Cleve, Leach is a threat,' Francome said, uncomfortable in his damp clothes and wriggling in the chair as he looked across the desk at Connor. 'We've got to do somethin' about him.'

'By "we" I presume you mean me,' Cleve Connor said. He was only half listening. His attention was focused on the article in *The Weekly Crossing* that Francome had brought him.

'Well, yes. An' Luke's only too anxious to put a bullet in him.'

Cleve tapped the newspaper. 'What's all this about?'

'Mm, what? Oh, that,' Francome said. 'It's the other thing Leach is fixed on findin' out more about. An' I guess while he's concentratin' on that he's not comin' after us.'

'Us? You, you mean. The only name he's got in his sights is Travis Newton, from what you tell me. That ain't me.'

Francome felt his anger swell up inside him. 'Might be just me at the moment, but a word from me an' he could be takin' an interest in you, too, Cleve. Don't forget that.'

Cleve's eyes turned to ice. 'Is that a threat, Ches?' he said in a quiet but deadly voice. 'Because you, of all people, should know by now what happens to folk who threaten me.'

'N-no, 'course not, Cleve,' Francome said, backing down quickly. 'I didn't . . . I mean it was a stupid . . .' His voice tailed away.

'Stupid, yeah,' Cleve said. 'An' dangerous.' He indicated the newspaper report again and adopted a more casual tone. 'You have any idea who this Jabal Hawley might be? Whether he's livin' here an' what name he might be hidin' under?'

Francome shook his head. 'Ain't got a clue.'

'Be useful to find out before Leach does,' Cleve said. 'Ask around. See what you can find out.'

'Sure, Cleve.' Francome was about to leave when he seemed to remember something. 'Didn't you mention Stokewood as one of the places you knew before the War?'

'Might have,' Cleve said. 'I don't recall. Went to a lot of different places before puttin' on a uniform an' gettin' shot at by a lot of Yankees.'

Francome was about to speak again and Cleve put up a hand to stop him. 'Yes, OK, I'll tell Luke it's time to take care of Leach.'

So it was a relieved Chesney Francome who headed back to Ox Crossing. Even the storm had passed and the sun had emerged, to add to his lightened mood.

Nat waited until the sheriff was out of sight before he made his way towards the ranch. He had decided it was time to talk with Cleve Connor, the man most people seemed to think was the instigator behind Joe Spearing's murder. And, after witnessing Francome's association with the rancher at first hand, Nat was also entertaining suspicions that Cleve Connor might be someone other than whom he professed to be. That both he and Francome could be the men Nat had been seeking since the end of the War between the States.

Connor had come out of the house to see Francome depart and had walked across to the corral to speak with the two ranch hands. So he became aware of Nat's arrival well before the latter reached the house. He had never met Nat, but something told him this was the man who was scaring the pants off Chesney Francome.

Minutes later he knew he had guessed right.

'The name's Nathan Leach,' Nat told him, dismounting alongside the corral. 'Mind if I take up a few minutes of your time, Mr Connor?'

'Sure. You'd better come into the house,' Connor replied, looking Nat over, and in particular at the six-gun Nat was carrying.

Nat noticed and smiled. 'I can leave my gun with one of your men if that makes you feel more comfortable.

Connor laughed. 'No need. I don't figure you're goin' to shoot me, not yet anyway.'

Nat dismounted and followed Connor into the house. They crossed a wide hallway where a long-case clock stood in an alcove, and on into what was evidently Connor's study.

'Take a seat,' Connor said, indicating the chair Francome had vacated earlier, then sitting down behind the desk. 'What can I do for you?' He tapped the copy of *The Weekly Crossing* on the desktop. 'If it's anythin' to do with this article in the paper, then I can't help you. The name Jabal Hawley means nothin' to me.'

'You ever meet my army buddy Joe Spearing?' Nat asked.

Connor shrugged. 'Not that I remember. Might've

passed the time of day with him in the Silver Buck. Seems he hung out there quite a bit. There or Angie Smith's whorehouse. Your army buddy was he?'

'He was. And he saved my life.'

'Guess that's reason enough to want to find out who killed him.'

'Any thoughts about the way he was killed?'

'Bushwhacked, wasn't he?'

'That's right.'

'Reckon he could've upset somebody then. Either that, or he was robbed. You spoken to Sheriff Francome about this?'

'Not yet, but I aim to.'

Connor shuffled the newspaper, then folded it up and dropped it on the floor beside him. 'Got anythin' else on your mind, anythin' I can help you with?'

'Matter of fact there is something,' Nat said. 'You ever heard the name Travis Newton?'

Connor shook his head. 'Can't say I have. You lookin' for him for a particular reason?'

'Yeah, I've got a reason,' Nat said. 'He and three other yellow-bellied confederate army deserters raped and killed my mother and sister.'

Some of the colour seemed to seep from Connor's face. 'Your mother and sister. That's . . . terrible.'

'Yeah,' Nat said.

They were silent for several moments, then Connor said, 'Too bad I can't be of any help, but I can understand why you'd want to find these four men.'

'Just two actually,' Nat told him. 'The other two – Brooks and Cutler – are dead.'

Connor's face remained expressionless.

'The army caught up with Cyrus Cutler and he was shot for desertion,' Nat continued. 'Eli Brooks died in Yuma prison, but not before he dropped me the name Travis Newton.'

Connor absorbed this information before asking, 'What about the fourth man? Did Brooks tell you that name, too?'

Nat shook his head. 'Said it would be better for my health if I didn't know. Best if I stopped looking for him altogether, he said. Seems he's a particularly dangerous *hombre*.'

'Might've been good advice then,' Connor said. 'I mean, if he's that dangerous.'

'Maybe,' Nat said. 'Doesn't change anything though. I'll keep looking for *both* of them.'

'An' if you find them?'

'Oh, I'll find them. And then I'll kill them,' Nat said, matter-of-factly.

The two men sat in silence again for several seconds, then Connor rose from his seat.

'Well, if that's all?' he said.

'For now,' Nat said, getting to his feet. 'If you should hear anything that might help me track down Newton, I'd be obliged if you'd contact me.'

'Sure, sure!' Connor said.

'Only from what I hear, you're a man of influence in the town,' Nat said. 'The sort of man people might confide in with their secrets. And from what I can gather, there's more than a few folk with secrets in Ox Crossing.'

'You think this Travis Newton might be willin' to give

you the name of the fourth man?'

'I reckon I should be able to persuade him to . . . before I put a bullet through his brain,' Nat said.

Connor looked at him with a thoughtful expression. 'Yeah, I reckon you might,' he said.

He followed Nat out to his horse. Neither man spoke again. Connor stood in the porch and watched Nat ride away.

'Where are you, Luke?' he muttered to himself. 'Seems I've got a chore for you. Maybe two chores, startin' with a loose-lipped sheriff.'

CHAPTER 12

Howard Ellis lit a cigar and offered one to the man sitting across the table from him. Otis Bream accepted the offer, and the two men lit up. They were at a corner table in the Ace Hotel restaurant. It was the bigger and more expensive of Ox Crossing's two hotels (and thus the reason Nat had avoided it). The remains of what had been a substantial lunch stood on the white linen tablecloth covering the table. Otis poured himself a second glass of brandy. A folded copy of *The Weekly Crossing* lay beside the coffee pot.

The two men smoked in silence for a minute or so before Howard tapped the newspaper.

'What's Gabe doing printing stories about an age-old crime in a place miles away?' he said.

'Beats me,' Otis said.

'It's got something to do with that young fellow – Leach, is his name? – who came to town a couple of days ago,' Howard said.

'Him and Angie Smith – er, so I'm told,' Otis added quickly.

Howard sighed. 'Really, Otis, you don't have to pretend

85

you don't pay regular visits to the town's best known whore. You're a widower, but nobody expects you to be celibate.'

Otis looked uncomfortable but said nothing.

'So Angie Smith had a hand in this report, did she?' Howard went on. 'Well, the young Spearing did keep her company whilst he was here. Maybe she took a shine to him, and that's the reason she hooked up with Leach and went to see Gabe. Helped Leach persuade him to run the story in the paper.'

'Toby Greenway wrote it, according to the byline,' Otis said.

'Gabe's grooming the youngster to take over the paper when he's retired,' Howard said.

'Toby's sweet on Lyle Walker's stepdaughter,' Otis said.

'Is he?' Howard said. 'Speaking of Lyle, he suddenly seems a lot more confident about winning the mayoral election. Have you heard anything, Otis?'

'Well, we both know whoever wins is going to need Cleve Connor's backing. Cleve has a lot of . . . influence in the town.'

' "Influence", yes, that's one way of putting it. People owe him, so they'll do as he tells them – if he can be bothered, that is.'

'Oh, he'll be bothered, Howard. As to Lyle Walker, maybe he knows something about Cleve that Cleve would rather keep quiet, and that gives him a way of . . . well . . .'

'Blackmailing him?' Howard said. 'Don't be afraid to call a spade a spade. And I think you could be right. After all, we all have our secrets, don't we, Otis?' he added, meaningfully.

His companion's face coloured up. 'Not me,' he said, and he took a hurried swig of coffee.

'Maybe I should pay Lyle a visit, see what I can find out,' Howard said. 'Unobtrusively, of course.'

'Might be better to have a confidential word with his wife,' Otis suggested.

Howard nodded. 'That's a good idea. D'you know, I'm not convinced Jane is all that keen on her husband becoming mayor, what with all the responsibility that goes with the job. She worries about Lyle's health. And she could have good reason. You remember Lyle had what seemed like a heart attack a few months ago? Doc Gorman told him to take things easier for a while and he'd be fine, but I know Jane gets anxious. Yes, I'll pay her a visit. Best wait until Lyle is out, though.'

Luke Trey waited until Nat Leach was well clear of the Circle C before gigging his mount forward and emerging from the stand of trees where he had been waiting. In spite of itching to put a bullet in the back of the other man, Luke resisted the temptation.

He found Cleve back in his study.

'You've had visitors, boss,' he said.

'You saw them?'

Luke nodded. 'Figured I'd wait until they'd gone. What did they want?'

'Francome's panickin', as you might expect,' Cleve said. 'You shootin' Jarvis didn't help any. I hope you were well paid.'

'How d'you know it was me? Could've been anybody.'

'Not only was *I* able to guess it was your handiwork, so

were a good number of other folk, accordin' to Francome,' Cleve said. 'Which is why he's gettin' hassled. He's also gettin' jumpy about the Leach fellah.'

'Why's that?' Luke asked, although he reckoned he knew the answer.

' 'Cause Leach is askin' too many awkward questions,' Cleve said.

'About Travis Newton an' our lily-livered sheriff?'

'Yeah. An' he's gettin' too close to the right answer.'

'That why Leach paid you a visit? To let you know that?'

'I ain't sure exactly what his reason was for comin' here. All I know is, Francome's a blabbermouth an' Leach is dangerous.' He looked directly at Luke. 'So I've got a coupla chores for you.'

'Reckon I can guess what they are without you tellin' me,' Luke said.

'All the same, I'll spell it out,' Cleve said.

And he did.

Talking about Angie Smith with Howard Ellis had left Otis with an urgent need of female company. So it was that, after leaving the hotel and watching Howard walk towards Lyle Walker's house, instead of going back to his real estate office, Otis drifted towards the Silver Buck where he thought he might find one of Angie's soiled doves touting for trade. Maybe he could discreetly signal that he was in the market for what she was offering without making it obvious to all and sundry.

In the event, it wasn't necessary. Angie herself was coming out of the saloon and seeing the furtive, and at the same time eager expression on Otis' face, guessed his intentions. So all it required was a smile and a raised eyebrow on her part to indicate that Otis should follow her to her house, after a suitable interval, and she would happily satisfy his needs.

A relieved Otis changed direction and walked to the mercantile where he purchased some unwanted tobacco. Then, making sure there was nobody paying attention to him, he walked quickly to Angie's house and went inside.

Angie was in the lobby talking to one of her girls.

'Go on up, sugar,' she said to Otis. 'You know the way. I'll be with you in a few minutes.'

Hurriedly, Otis climbed the steep winding staircase. He was a short, stout little man and was quite out of breath by the time he reached the door of Angie's room. He let himself in and sat panting on the side of the large four-poster bed. Angie joined him a minute or two later.

'My, Otis, you're out of condition,' she said, seeing him puffing. 'Are you sure you're up to this? We don't want you having a heart attack, do we? Could be kinda embarrassing.'

'I'll . . . I'll be fine in a few . . . minutes,' Otis gasped.

'Well, let's just chat for a spell,' Angie suggested. 'Let you get your breath back. Then we can get down to things.'

Otis nodded.

'Saw you with Howard Ellis earlier,' Angie said. 'Now there's a man who – well, best not go into that. You going to vote for him in the mayoral election?'

Otis nodded again.

They sat quietly for a while, then Angie said, 'Terrible thing about Cliff Jarvis. What d'you think's going on, Otis?

I mean, first it was poor Joe Spearing, and now Cliff. Got to be a connection, don't you think?'

'Possibly,' Otis said, carefully.

'Of course, Cliff always knew things about people,' Angie said. She looked directly at Otis. 'Things they wouldn't want spread around.'

Otis began to look uncomfortable. 'Yes, well. . . .'

'Did you read the article Toby Greenway wrote in the paper?' Angie asked. 'The one about the Stokewood killer, Jabal Hawley?'

'Yes, I read it,' Otis said.

'Nat Leach, who suggested Gabe should print the article, was a friend of Joe Spearing. They were army buddies.'

'I thought it was you who persuaded Gabe,' Otis said.

'Well, I guess it was both of us. Anyway, it seems likely Joe saw Jabal Hawley here in Ox Crossing, and maybe that's why he was killed.'

'It seems a bit far-fetched to me,' Otis said. 'And even if Spearing did see Jabal Hawley then, it's no guarantee he's still in town.'

'Maybe not,' Angie said, looking carefully at him. 'I'd never heard of Stokewood before Joe spoke of it. Have you heard of it?'

'Uh – I might have,' Otis said.

'But not Jabal Hawley,' Angie said.

'No, of course not. Why would I?' He took off his jacket. 'Anyway, can we. . . ?'

Angie responded by starting to unbutton her dress. 'Yes, of course. You didn't come to see me just for a chat, did you Otis?'

CHAPTER 13

Jane Walker was taken aback to see Howard Ellis standing outside when she answered the knocking on her door.

'Howard!' she said, greeting her husband's opponent in the race to be mayor with a surprised smile. 'What brings you here? I'm afraid Lyle's out. He had a meeting at the bank and I don't expect him back any time soon.'

Howard returned her smile. 'Actually, Jane, it was you I wanted to speak with.'

'Really?' she said, with a little laugh. 'How mysterious. Well, you'd better come in.'

He followed her into the hallway, past doors leading to the kitchen and a study and into a large living room bathed in sunlight. It overlooked an immaculate stretch of grass surrounded by flowering shrubs.

'I'm all alone in the house,' Jane said. 'Pattie, our maid, has the afternoon off, and Molly is at the school. She helps out two or three days each week. She loves working with the children and has a hankering to be a teacher.'

'I'm sure she'd make an excellent teacher,' Howard said. 'She's a talented young lady.'

'Lyle wouldn't hear of it. "She can do better for herself than being a school ma-arm" he says. "That's a job for old maids." '

Howard laughed. 'He may have a point. Anyway, from what I hear, Molly and young Toby Greenway have an "understanding", so she's unlikely to become an old maid.'

Jane sighed. 'And that was something of a bone of contention between Lyle and Molly, until recently, but thankfully I think Lyle's altering his opinion of the young man – for the better, I mean. Anyway, what was it you wanted to see me about, Howard? If it's to do with the mayoral election you'll be putting me in an invidious position.'

'Well, it's not directly about the election,' Howard said. 'More to do with Lyle's health.'

Jane looked suddenly alarmed. 'Have you heard something? Has Lyle told you something he hasn't told me?'

'Not Lyle, no,' Howard said, carefully. 'I was chatting with Doc Gorman the other day. Now you mustn't tell the Doc I've mentioned this to you, but Doc confided in me that he was worried about the strain the election campaign was putting on Lyle's heart. Also, about the responsibility the mayor's job would incur if he won the election, and the effect it would have on Lyle's health.'

Jane shook her head. 'Lyle is adamant. He says he's fine now.'

'Well, if he's sure. It's not long since he had his heart attack, is it?' As he said this, something occurred to Howard. 'February, wasn't it? Around the time that Spearing man was killed.'

'February, yes,' Jane said.

'Tell me, did Lyle know Joe Spearing? I seem to recall he paid Lyle a visit.'

Jane shrugged. 'He may have. I really couldn't say.'

'No matter,' Howard said. He paused for a moment, then went on. 'Of course, both Lyle and myself need Cleve Connor's backing to win the election, we both know that.'

'Is that right?' Jane looked as if she was anxious to be rid of her visitor but didn't quite know how to achieve it.

Howard decided to try a stab in the dark. 'He's been to see Cleve, hasn't he? With some ... information. Something that may sway the vote in his direction.'

'He ... may have,' Jane said, evasively. 'I really don't know. He doesn't discuss these things with me, Howard.'

Her hesitation told Howard all he needed to know. *The bastard has got something on Connor and he's twisting Cleve's arm.* 'Well, I'll be getting along,' he said. 'I just thought you ought to know what Doc Gorman said.'

'Thank you, Howard,' Jane replied, following him to the door.

There was a copy of *The Weekly Crossing* on a table in the hallway. Howard gestured towards it. 'Have you read Toby Greenway's article about the Stokewood killing and its possible connection with Joe Spearing's murder?' he said.

Jane shook her head. 'I haven't looked at the newspaper yet.'

'It makes interesting reading. Didn't Lyle have some friend or relative in Stokewood?'

'No, I'm sure he didn't,' Jane said. 'I've never heard him mention the place, or Jabal Hawley.'

Howard gave her a strange look. 'You know the name

Jabal Hawley? Only you said you hadn't read the article yet. So where else would you have heard it?'

Jane became flustered. 'Really, Howard! I've no idea. Why all the questions?'

She was trying to contain her annoyance, but it was clear to Howard that he had disconcerted her. He was about to say something more when Molly appeared in the kitchen doorway that led off the hall. She had obviously come in the back entrance.

'Hello, Molly,' he said. 'How were things at the school today?'

'Fine, Mr Ellis,' she replied.

'Going to the church social tonight?' he asked.

Molly nodded. 'Yes.' She looked at her mother. 'Toby is calling for me at seven.' And she went through to the living room before either of them could say anything more.

But Howard wondered how much of his conversation with her mother she had overheard.

94

CHAPTER 14

Luke stretched out flat on the rooftop of the mercantile and eased himself into a comfortable position. He had secured his vantage point without anyone noticing him, using two empty barrels at the rear of the building as leverage in his climb to the roof. It was almost seven-thirty and stars were beginning to appear in the darkening sky. He wasn't sure how long he would have to wait for one or both of his targets to emerge from the Silver Buck opposite. He had observed them both enter the saloon separately more than an hour ago.

The street below was almost empty – just an occasional straggler making his way to Freda's eating house or the saloon. Luke considered what he knew or had guessed about the situation he found himself embroiled in. One thing he was certain of: Cleve Connor was a nervous man – almost as nervous as the man who had paid Luke to kill Cliff Jarvis. And although he had the feeling each man's reason for wanting their respective target disposed of was the same – to stop a secret being revealed – he wasn't sure if it was the same secret. He cursed himself for not trying

95

to read the wire Cliff Jarvis had been carrying. Reading was something Luke struggled with, but maybe could have made out enough to have given him some answers.

Three men came out of the saloon at the same time. They paused on the boardwalk in front of the batwing doors to continue a spirited conversation that had started inside. A few seconds later, Nat Leach came out behind them. The three men seemed keen to engage him in their conversation and he seemed ready to join in.

Luke nestled his Winchester against his shoulder and waited for the three men to move into a position which gave him a clear sight of Leach. At last they seemed ready to go their different ways.

Luke took aim.

Nat heard the bark of the rifle a split second after its bullet splintered the boardwalk upright next to him. It had been a near thing – so near that a sliver of wood embedded itself in Nat's left cheek as he threw himself down on to the boards. He slithered into a position behind a drinking trough and some tethered horses, and looked up at the rooftops opposite.

Another rifle shot that hit the water trough pinpointed the shooter's position for him: the roof of the mercantile. But even as he determined this, he saw the shadowy figure of a man retreat to the back of the building, clearly having decided to abandon the assassination attempt until another time.

Nat scrambled to his feet and ran across the street. But by the time he reached the alleyway at the side of the store, the shooter had vanished. Not that Nat had any doubts about who had tried to kill him. It would be Luke Trey. But why? To avenge the humiliation Nat had caused him the first day by taking away Trey's gun? Or was he in the pay of someone else, his boss Cleve Connor for instance?

The three men he'd been talking with outside the saloon had scattered, but two of the three came back to check on him and noted his bloody face.

'You OK?' one of them asked.

'He get away?'

'Yes, and yes,' Nat told them, pulling off his neckerchief and using it to stem the flow of blood coming from his cheek.

At that moment, Sheriff Francome came out of the saloon.

'What'n hell's goin' on?' he demanded. 'Who's doin' all the shootin'?'

'Marksman on the roof of the mercantile,' one of the two men answered. 'Took a potshot at our friend here. Missed, thankfully.'

Francome looked at Nat. 'Any idea who it was?'

Nat shook his head. 'No.'

But I'd lay odds you know.

'Too bad,' Francome said. 'Best watch your back then.'

'I'll do that, *Travis*,' Nat said.

'OK, then I'll – what did you call me?' Francome's face had paled.

'Sheriff,' Nat said. This was not the time for a direct accusation, Francome would just deny it. Better to keep him rattled for the time being. 'I called you sheriff. What did you think I called you?'

The two men stared at each other for a moment, then the lawman walked away.

And Nat was now certain he'd found one of the two men he'd been searching for.

Chap Fancy was playing solitaire on Francome's desk when the sheriff entered. The lawman was muttering to himself.

'*He knows. The bastard knows.*'

Chap looked up. 'Who knows?' he asked. 'Knows what?'

'Mm?' Francome became aware of his deputy's presence. 'What? Oh, nothin'. That critter Leach just got shot at. Reckoned the shooter was on the roof of the mercantile.'

'You get him? The shooter, I mean?'

'No, he got away after takin' a coupla shots.'

'Where was Leach when he came under fire?'

'Comin' out of the Silver Buck. He'd been playin' poker with three other men an' he followed them out. I saw him leave.'

'You were in the saloon?'

'Yeah, what about it?'

'Thought you were doin' the rounds, checkin' on things,' Chap said.

'Well I wasn't!' Francome growled. 'I was gonna do it after I came out.'

'But Leach said somethin' that kinda put you off your stride,' Chap said, a twinkle in his eye.

'Yes. No! Figured I'd leave the rounds for another half-hour.' He motioned for Chap to remove himself from his chair, then occupied it himself. He opened a desk drawer and withdrew a bottle of red eye and a glass. He poured

98

himself a drink and downed it in one.

Chap gathered up his playing cards and walked across to the window. 'Seems quiet enough now. You want me to. . . ?'

'Yes!' Francome snapped. 'Go do it.'

Chap took his gunbelt from one of the hooks on the wall and strapped it on. He seemed about to say something else, but changed his mind. Instead, he went out into the street where all was quiet after the earlier excitement.

Chap began to stroll along the boardwalk, checking on doors but with his mind elsewhere. What was it exactly that Ches Francome was afraid of? What was it Leach thought he knew about him? Chap was sure the two were connected.

Then he remembered Leach had asked about a *hombre* with the name of Travis Newton, and when Chap had mentioned this to Francome it had unsettled him. Why? Because *he* was Newton? It sounded like a name Ches muttered in his sleep sometimes when he dozed off in the office.

And if Ches *was* Newton, what had he done? Why would he be hiding away in Ox Crossing under a false name?

Chap had reached Freda's eating house and decided to have himself a cup of coffee and maybe a slice of Freda's pumpkin pie. He was in no hurry to get back to the sheriff's office, not with Ches bitching about everything.

There was only one other customer in the café: Luke Trey. He sat in a corner, his back to the wall so that he could see whoever entered. He was working his way through a plate of stew. Chap noticed a flicker of apprehension in Trey's expression when he saw the deputy come in, but it was gone in an instant.

Chap nodded to him, then found himself a table. Freda came across and Chap gave his order.

'What was all the shooting about earlier?' she asked him in a low voice.

'Somebody took a coupla potshots at the Leach guy,' Chap said. 'Missed, though. So not much of a marksman. Guess he should've crept up on him an' shot him in the back.' He was aware his words were being heard by the other occupant of the room. Indeed, that was his intention. Because Chap reckoned there was a good chance Trey was the culprit and goading him just might make him give himself away. Dangerous tactics, though. A bit like tugging a tiger's tail, Chap thought to himself.

But Trey continued to eat in silence until his plate was empty. He tossed some coins on the table and pushed his chair back. He stood up, gave Chap a long, hard look, then left.

Chap let out a relieved sigh. But that look had been enough to convince him he'd discovered the identity of the sniper. But proving it was another matter. What was more, there was little point in telling Ches, he reflected. Trey worked for Cleve Connor, and the sheriff would never make trouble for Connor, even if it could be proved Trey had been working under Connor's orders. Connor had 'bought and paid for' Francome a long time ago, everybody knew that.

But that raised another question in Chap's mind: if Trey had been acting on behalf of Connor, why would Connor want Leach dead? Something to do with the Stokewood report in the newspaper?

Maybe it was time for him to have a private word with Leach, Chap thought.

CHAPTER 15

The wooden church hall at the back of the church was too far from the main street for anyone to be aware of the shooting. Besides which, there was a hubbub of music, chatter and laughter that would drown out any noise of gunshots.

Toby and Molly sat at one end of the hall with plates of food on their laps. Whilst Toby was making headway with his, Molly was just picking at hers in an abstracted manner.

'Something on your mind, Molly?' Toby asked between mouthfuls.

'Mm? Oh, it's nothing really,' she replied.

'Whatever it is, it seems to be spoiling your appetite.'

'It's just. . . .'

'Go on.' Toby put his plate on the empty seat next to him. 'Maybe I can help.'

'It's something I overheard this afternoon,' Molly said. 'I'd been at the school and I'd just arrived home. As usual, I went into the house through the back entrance to get a glass of water from the kitchen.' She chuckled. 'Working with kids always seems to give me a thirst. Anyway, I heard voices in the hall and realized Howard Ellis was talking with Mother.'

'Probably trying to find out how your step-pa's election campaign is going,' Toby said.

'Perhaps. But he was asking her about your report in *The Weekly Crossing*.'

'Really?' Toby was surprised, but also quite pleased that his article had aroused the interest of the mayor.

'Yes. Well, Ma said she hadn't read it yet. But Mr Ellis seemed to think my stepfather knew somebody in Stokewood at one time. Mother said she was sure he didn't and that she'd never heard him mention the place or Jabal Hawley. To which *he* replied, "You know the name Jabal Hawley? Only you said you hadn't read the article yet. So where else would you have heard it?" '

Toby frowned. 'What did your mother say?'

'Nothing. Because it was then that they noticed me in the kitchen doorway, and Mr Ellis left a minute or two later.'

'So what are you worried about?' Toby asked.

'It was only later, when I remembered something,' Molly said. 'A few months ago I heard my stepfather talking with my mother, and I'm sure I heard the name Stokewood mentioned. Anyway, I asked her about it before you called for me this evening.'

'What did she say?'

'She got quite angry, and denied ever having the conversation between herself and my stepfather about Stokewood or whether he knew anybody there.'

'But you're sure it took place?'

'Yes. So now I'm wondering why Mother lied to me and Mr Ellis.'

Toby looked thoughtful. 'You say this conversation took place a few months ago. Can you be more precise?'

'Why?'

'I just wondered . . . was it before or after Joe Spearing was killed?'

Molly looked shocked. 'What are you saying? That my stepfather and mother knew something to do with Joey Spearing's murder?' She stood up quickly, forgetting the plate of food on her lap. It fell to the floor with a clatter, causing several people to look round. 'Toby Greenway, that's a terrible thing to say! Do you really believe. . . ?'

Toby put a placatory hand on her arm, drew her down on her chair again, and stooped to pick up her plate. 'I'm sorry. But, Molly – well – it does sound as though your mother knew the name Jabal Hawley from somewhere. Maybe Joe Spearing mentioned his suspicions to her or your stepfather before he was killed.'

'About Hawley's new identity?'

'Perhaps.'

'Then why wouldn't they have told Sheriff Francome? It would have explained much earlier why Spearing was killed.'

'Perhaps because Francome *is* Hawley. He's about the right age.'

Molly blinked rapidly. 'Is he?' She shook her head. 'No, they'd have told *someone*. My mother is an old friend of Judge Parsons. They would have gone to him with the information.'

They sat in an awkward silence for several minutes,

104

each avoiding the other's glance. By this time, everyone had finished eating, and dancing was about to begin. Toby cursed himself for upsetting the love of his life when all he wanted to do was take her in his arms and kiss her. But the companionable mood of earlier was broken and it was going to take him the rest of the evening to restore it. Damn that article! He was wishing he'd never written it.

Nat went back to his hotel room to remove the splinter in his cheek and clean up the split skin. He had just finished doing this when, passing by the window, he saw Luke Trey emerge from Freda's café and walk towards the saloon. He must have disposed of his Winchester somewhere because he wasn't carrying it, Nat noticed. Maybe he'd left it with the bartender at the Silver Buck, as they seemed to be on friendly terms. Maybe that was why Trey was heading there now, to retrieve it.

'And maybe it's time that *hombre* and I had another meeting,' Nat muttered to himself. 'But on more equal terms.'

Luke Trey found himself a space at the bar and indicated to the barkeep that he wanted a drink. A glass of whiskey appeared in front of him seconds later. The barkeep raised his eyebrows in question but Luke shook his head. *No, I don't want my Winchester right now.*

The saloon was busy with drinkers, card players and a handful of soiled doves plying for trade. Luke looked to see if Angie Smith was amongst them, but she was not. A man in a spangled waistcoat played on a badly tuned honky-tonk piano.

A few heads turned in the direction of the batwing doors and Luke glanced round in time to see Nat Leach enter the bar. Leach looked around until he saw Luke, then made a beeline for him. Luke straightened up and let his hand drop casually to the holster at his side, glad that he had replaced the firearm that was still in the sheriff's custody. The move did not go unnoticed, either by Leach or a good number of other people. Several men who had been either side of Luke suddenly made space around him and found somewhere else to stand or sit.

Nat signalled to the bartender and perched on a bar stool a couple of feet from Trey. 'Give me a beer,' he said. His words were addressed to the barkeep but his eyes remained on Luke.

Luke returned the stare.

The barkeep placed the tankard of foaming liquid in front of Nat, then said, 'If you two have a hankerin' to settle some argument, I'd appreciate it if you'd settle it outside.'

'I don't reckon Mr Trey would risk a face-off,' Nat said. 'He prefers to *settle* things from a rooftop and under cover of darkness. That right, Trey? Want to tell me whose orders you were carrying out? Or maybe you were acting on your own behalf?'

'Don't know what you're talkin' about.' Luke took a swig from his glass and made as if to move away from the bar.

'You keeping anything for Mr Trey, barkeep?' Nat asked. 'Like a Winchester, maybe?'

It was a wild shot, but it found its target. The barkeep's facial expression of fear and confusion was enough to

106

confirm what Nat had guessed.

'No damn business of yours what I leave with him!' Luke growled. 'Yeah, he's got my Winchester. So what? It leaves me with my hands free if'n I want to play poker or enjoy the company of a woman.'

'Mind if I see it?' Nat asked. 'Check if it's been fired recently?'

'Yeah, I mind,' Luke said. 'You can take my word for it. It ain't been fired in a week.'

Nat swallowed a mouthful of beer. He looked into the other man's eyes. 'I don't believe you,' he said.

Luke's face flushed. 'You callin' me a liar?'

'Guess I am,' Nat said. 'You got anything to say about that?'

'I'll let my gun do the talkin', that's what!' Luke said.

'Not in here!' the barkeep reminded them.

'Outside, Leach!' Luke growled, and marched unsteadily towards the batwings. 'If'n you've got the guts.'

Nat drained his tankard before sliding off the bar stool and following him into the street. A small crowd of onlookers went after them, jostling for vantage points on the boardwalk to watch the confrontation.

'You sure about this, Trey?' Nat asked, stepping out into the night and adopting a fifteen-yard space between himself and Luke. 'You could be about to meet your Maker. Or more likely, the devil.'

'Sure I'm sure, you bastard!' Luke drawled. 'Draw!' And he went for his gun.

It had barely cleared its holster before a bloody hole appeared dead centre of Luke's head and he corkscrewed to the ground with a surprised expression on his face.

A collective gasp came from the onlookers, together with mutterings of 'Jeeze, did you see that?' and 'How'n hell did he get to be that fast? He some gunslinger?'

Deputy Chap Fancy had been hurrying from the café, alerted by the crowd forming that something was about to happen. But he was too late to stop the shooting.

'What happened, Leach?' he asked as he looked down at Trey's motionless body.

'Guess he wanted to finish what he failed to do earlier,' Nat said.

Chap sighed and looked around. 'Anybody here want to say who went for his weapon first?'

'Trey did,' came a voice from the throng, and this was accompanied by mutterings of agreement.

'Even so,' Chap said to Nat, 'I'd best take your gun until we've had a word with Sheriff Francome. He'll want a fuller explanation.' He looked around again. 'Anybody seen Ches?'

There was no answer until a voice said, 'He'll be keepin' his head down, as usual when there's trouble.' This was greeted with a round of chuckles and mutterings of agreement.

'OK, OK!' Ches growled. 'Somebody go fetch the undertaker.'

He moved to take Nat's gun, but something in the other man's eyes stopped him. 'Oh well, I guess you ain't plannin' on shootin' anybody else just now. Let's go.'

Francome had witnessed the killing from his office window further along the street. As the anonymous joker from the crowd had indicated, Francome had indeed decided to keep out of things, for the simple reason that he had expected – hoped – that Luke Trey would be faster on the draw and would thus eliminate the man whom he, Francome, had come to fear. But it hadn't happened. And now Chap was bringing the damn Leach man to the office to explain all. Francome didn't want to hear it. He was already dreading the trip to the Circle C to tell Cleve Connor what had happened to his henchman. He reckoned there'd be hell to pay, and that he'd get more than his fair share of the blame.

The street door opened, and Chap and Leach came in.

'Ah, there you are, Ches,' Chap said, unable to keep the sarcasm out of his voice. 'Folks were wonderin' where you'd got to.'

'I was about to come, then I saw you had it all under control,' Francome said. He looked at Leach. 'Trouble seems to follow you around, mister.'

'Just one source of trouble,' Nat said. 'And now he's dead.'

'Witnesses say it was a fair fight, Ches,' Chap said. 'Trey drew first – or tried to. Leach here was faster.'

'What was the argument about?' Francome asked.

'The earlier shooting,' Nat said. 'Trey was the rooftop sniper. I'm guessing he might've been acting on Cleve Connor's orders. But I reckon you knew that.'

'What in hell d'you mean, you reckon I knew it?' Francome challenged. 'How could I?'

'Because folks around here say you're Connor's man,' Nat said. 'And when you make a point of steering clear of any trouble Connor's chief honcho is causing, it gets me thinking they're right. That you were expecting – *hoping* even – that Trey was going to make a move on me.'

Francome was aware of Chap listening closely to what was being said, and he was beginning to fear Leach was about to bring the name Travis Newton into the discussion.

'You finish doin' the rounds afore you went to Freda's café?' he asked his deputy.

'Er – almost,' Chap said.

'Go finish 'em,' Francome told him. 'I'll handle this critter.'

Chap glanced at Nat. 'OK,' he said, before heading out of the door.

When they were alone, Francome said, 'Seein' as there were witnesses sayin' you weren't to blame, I won't take this no further. But best thing you can do is clear out of Ox Crossin' first thing in the mornin' an' don't come back.'

Nat smiled. 'I make you nervous, don't I, Francome?' he said. 'No, let's call you by the name your ma and pa gave you: Travis Newton.'

'That's a lie!' Francome shouted.

'I don't think it is,' Nat said.

'Anyway, what is it about this Newton *hombre*? Why're you so all-fired anxious to find him?' Sweat was breaking out on Francome's face. 'What's he done to rile you?'

'Ask Connor, he'll tell you,' Nat said. 'And while you're about it, tell him I'm beginning to think he's the fourth confederate deserter. And when I'm *completely* sure . . . I'm going to kill the both of you.'

Nat turned, opened the door of the office and went out into the moonlit street.

'"Fourth man? Confederate deserter?" What'n

hell. . . ?' Francome started to say. Then realization hit him like a freight train coming out of a fog. With it, his face paled and he felt a damp patch spreading around his crotch. 'Oh, Jesus!'

Unable to restrain his curiosity after leaving the office, Chap had sneaked round to the rear door of the building and quietly let himself into the back room, where he had overheard the conversation between the two men. Now he let out the breath he'd been holding during the last thirty seconds.

'Well, I'll be damned!' he muttered to himself. 'You'd best watch out for yourself, Ches. That young man means business.'

CHAPTER 16

A dejected Toby Greenway made his way home after seeing a subdued Molly to her door. The goodnight kiss she had given him had, at best, been perfunctory. It seemed she had not forgiven him for suggesting her mother and stepfather might know something about the Spearing killing, and possibly the identity of Jabal Hawley.

He was roused from his preoccupations at the sight of a crowd breaking up outside the saloon. Something had happened, and his newspaperman's instinct kicked in. He put a hand on the arm of a passer-by and stalled him.

'What's going on?'

'That Leach fellah just shot Luke Trey,' the man said, unable to keep the excitement out of his voice. 'Jeeze, he was fast! Trey never had a chance.'

The man walked on before Toby could ask any more. A moment later, he saw Gabe Crighton amongst the remnants of the crowd. He was asking questions, a notebook and pencil in his hands. The editor was doing his job.

Toby joined him.

'I just got here,' he said. 'What exactly happened, Gabe?'

Gabe related what he'd learned, finishing with, 'It was Trey who drew first, and there were witnesses, so Francome had to let Nat Leach go.'

'You going to write up a report?'

Gabe nodded. 'Going back to the office now. Thought I'd write it whilst it was still fresh in my mind.' He tapped his notebook. 'Got a few onlookers' accounts. You know how folk like to see their name in the paper.'

'Think I'll come back to the office with you,' Toby said. 'I don't feel much like sleeping.'

Gabe studied Toby's glum expression. 'Thought you and Molly were going to the church social. Can't be over yet, surely. It's barely nine-thirty.'

'We left early. Molly wasn't . . . feeling well,' Toby said, his face reddening.

'Come on, Toby,' Gabe said. 'What really happened? I can see you're not happy about something.'

Toby sighed. 'You know me too well.'

'Out with it, then,' Gabe said.

Toby told him as they walked to the newspaper office, ending with, 'And now I wish I'd never written the damn article.'

Gabe opened the office door and Toby followed him inside. The newspaper editor had stayed silent whilst Toby had told his story, but now he said, 'So the question is, does Lyle Walker – and possibly Jane – know the identity of Jabal Hawley? And if so, why are they keeping it to themselves?'

'And asking that was what got me into trouble with Molly,' Toby said.

'Yes, I can see how it would,' Gabe said, thoughtfully.

'Of course there's one person Lyle Walker would keep quiet for if it could be put to his advantage.'

'Who?'

'Cleve Connor has a lot of votes he can call on for the mayoral election, if he chooses. Or if he was *persuaded*.'

'By Lyle Walker, in exchange for Lyle keeping quiet about Connor being Hawley, you mean. You think Connor is Hawley?'

'I don't know, but it's something to consider. Anyway, I need to write up the report about tonight's shooting.'

'Guess I'll leave you to it,' Toby said, glumly.

'Listen, don't worry about Molly,' Gabe told him. 'She'll come round. True love never runs smooth, and all that. And she does love you, I'm sure of that.'

'I hope you're right,' Toby said. 'See you tomorrow.'

News of Luke Trey's death reached Cleve Connor an hour after the killing, via one of his ranch hands who had been in the Silver Buck and had witnessed events.

'The Leach man accused Luke of tryin' to kill him earlier,' the ranch hand said. 'From a rooftop! Luke denied it, an' Leach called him a liar. So Luke had to . . .'

'Yeah, I get it, Lol,' Cleve said, angrily. 'You don't have to spell it out. The damn fool!'

'But why would Luke want to kill Leach?' Lol said. 'If'n he *was* the man on the rooftop. I guess somebody could've been payin' him. Luke hired out his gun on more'n one occasion.'

'Just forget it, Lol.'

'Could've been anybody on that roof,' Lol went on. 'Didn't have to be Luke.'

'*I said forget it!*' Cleve snarled.

'Sorry, boss,' Lol said. 'Guess I'll get me some shuteye.'

Cleve watched the man head for the bunkhouse, then began pacing his study. He lit a cigar and was annoyed to notice his hands were shaking. Luke dead, the Leach man was putting two and two together and making a correct four – damn it, things were going to hell in a handcart.

He was sitting at his desk brooding, the cigar smoked down to a butt, when he heard the sound of a horse drawing up outside the ranch house.

Francome.

Cleve wasn't surprised. He had been expecting the lily-livered lawman who had more than outlived his usefulness and was threatening to be Cleve's nemesis. But with Luke gone, the remedy was now in Cleve's hands, and his alone. And something needed to be done. Urgently. Before Francome blabbed to Leach and unleashed a storm of retribution.

The sheriff burst into the study without knocking.

'You heard, Cleve?' He was red in the face and there was a dark stain on the front of his pants.

'Yeah, I heard,' Cleve said.

'What're we gonna do? He knows for certain who I am, an' he said to tell you he reckons you're the "fourth confederate deserter". Is he talkin' about the time the four of us . . . when we . . .'

'Yeah, he is.'

'Shit! How come he's. . . ?'

'The women were his sister an' his ma,' Cleve cut in.

Francome's mouth dropped open and he sank down in the chair on the opposite side of Cleve's desk. 'Oh, God!'

'Reckon it's a mite late for askin' Him to help,' Cleve said.

'Yeah, reckon you're right,' Francome said. His hands were shaking. 'So what're we gonna do?'

'That's the second time you've asked that, an' I still don't have an answer,' Cleve said. ' 'Ceptin' to finish what Luke failed to do. You fancy the job?'

Francome shook his head. 'Can't say I do.'

'No, I thought not.'

'I'll do it if there's nobody else,' Francome said. 'But I figured you would . . .'

'Yeah, well you figured wrong,' Cleve said. 'I don't aim to get into a shoot-out with the critter. From what I hear, he's fast.'

Francome nodded. 'He is.'

'OK,' Cleve said. 'I need to think about it. Anyway, you'd best get back to town. And stay clear of any more conversations with Leach before you talk yourself into trouble.'

'OK, Cleve. But we need to do somethin' soon.'

Minutes later, Cleve watched the lawman ride away, a thoughtful expression on his face.

'The only thing I need to do soon is shut you up for good, Travis,' he said to himself.

Francome went straight to his office after leaving the Circle C. Chap had returned from his 'rounds' and was sitting in Francome's chair reading his dime novel.

'Where've you been, Ches?' Chap asked, knowing full well that his boss had been to bleat his woes to Cleve Connor.

'Never you mind,' Francome growled. 'I'm here now, so you can get along home.'

Chap eased himself from the chair. 'OK, Ches. You sure you're gonna be all right?'

'I'm fine. Just go,' Francome said.

So you can drink yourself into a stupor.

Chap decided it was best not to voice his thoughts. Instead, he went out into the night and headed home to his cabin.

Francome slumped into the vacated chair and took out the bottle of red eye and a glass. He was about to pour himself a drink when he saw something through the window that checked him. It was Angie Smith leaving the saloon and heading back to her house. She looked, he thought, particularly enticing tonight.

Suddenly, Francome's craving for alcohol transmuted into one of lust.

CHAPTER 17

Angie had been surprised to see Sheriff Francome hanging furtively outside her house when she opened her door shortly after she had returned from the saloon. But it was clear enough what he had in mind, so she had invited him in. Business was business, after all.

A half hour later, his needs satisfied, he seemed reluctant to leave.

'Something on your mind, Ches?' Angie asked.

Francome lay back and stared at the ceiling.

'You know me, Ches. I can be discreet if there's something you want to get off your chest.' Angie trailed her finger down that part of his body as if to emphasize the point.

'Yeah, I guess you can, Angie.' He turned towards her. 'But just how friendly are you with Leach? That's what I need to know.'

Alarm bells started ringing in Angie's head. 'Leach? He's nothing special,' she lied.

'Thought he was a friend of yours,' Francome said.

'He's an ... acquaintance. You're a friend, Ches,

there's a difference.' Angie almost choked on the words, but she sensed there was something important that Francome might be prepared to tell her. Something that might be a threat to Nat. In which case, she was prepared to swallow her pride and lie. 'Why? Is there something you've done that would give him a reason for coming after you? Something bad?'

'It happened a long time ago,' Francome said. 'Durin' the war. Everythin' was different when you didn't know if'n you were going to survive the next day. You . . . did things you wouldn't do in peacetime.'

'What sort of things?' Angie asked, although she suspected she knew the answer. 'You mean . . . with women? Taking advantage?'

Francome looked startled. 'How'd you know that?'

Angie shrugged. 'It's the sort of thing that happens in wartime.' She swallowed the bile that was rising in her throat as she forced herself to sound casual. 'And was the woman somebody Leach knew?'

Francome nodded. 'Things just got a bit out of hand, Angie. We never mean to hurt them.'

' "We?" "Them?" Are you saying there was more than one of you, and more than one woman?'

'I – I ain't sayin' any more.' He was sweating.

'You killed them, didn't you? The women, I mean.' Angie couldn't keep the disgust out of her voice.

'It was an accident,' Francome bleated.

'And Leach is getting close to finding out you were one of the men.'

'Yeah, he's a nosy bastard,' Francome said. 'And because of that his time's runnin' out.'

119

'You mean you're going to *kill* him?'

'Not me, someone else.'

'Who?'

Francome tapped the side of his nose, an artful look in his eye. 'For me to know an' you to guess at. Although it probably ain't healthy for you to guess, right. Let's just say a friend of mine.'

Cleve Connor, Angie thought. It had to be. Francome didn't have that many friends. In fact, come to think of it, Angie couldn't name one. Even Connor only befriended him for his own ends.

'Why would this "friend" be prepared to kill Mr Leach? Was he one of the "others" who attacked the women?'

'Yeah,' Francome admitted. 'An' he doesn't want Leach gettin' close to findin' out about him. Startin' with findin' out his real name, not the one he's usin' now.'

And I bet he's worried about you letting something slip when you're drunk. Angie eased herself into a sitting position in the bed, exposing her bare breasts. It was a calculated move. Francome's eyes turned towards them, as Angie had known they would.

'Who is he, Ches?' Angie said, taking his hand and putting it on her breast. 'You know me, I love secrets.' She giggled seductively.

Francome began massaging her breast. His breathing quickened.

'I – I can't tell you, Angie. He'd kill me if he found out.'

Angie took his hand and directed it under the covers. 'Come on, Ches. Cleve's a friend of mine, too. I won't say anything.'

Panic took over from lust and Francome froze. 'Who

says I'm talkin' about Cleve?' he said. 'Jeeze, Angie, you've got to . . .'

Angie put her free hand across his lips. 'Take it easy. This is just between the two of us. What's Cleve's real name? What is it?' she said softly.

'It's . . . Jess Taggart,' Francome said, his breath coming more quickly by the second. 'But you have to keep it to yourself, Angie. Promise me!'

'What? Oh, sure,' Angie said. Then a thought struck her. 'I thought you were going to tell me it was Hawley, the man who got written about in the paper. The one from Stokewood.'

'What? No. Well, he could be him, too,' Francome said. She could feel him become aroused again and he pulled her back down under the bedcovers.

'What do you mean?' Angie was determined to get all the information out of him she could before she succumbed to his cravings.

'I didn't know Cleve before the war,' Francome said. 'But he did say somethin' about being in Stokewood at one time.'

'Living there?'

'Jeeze, I don't know!' He gave a grunt of exasperation. 'Hell, Angie, just forget about it! I need some more pleasurin'!'

And I need to talk to Nat, and soon! Angie thought.

Cleve Connor used the back entrance to the sherriff's office. It was never locked. He made his way in the semi-darkness through the room where Francome slept and into the front office. It was empty.

'I can wait, Ches,' he muttered to himself.

And then, glancing through the window, he saw the familiar shape of the lawman making his way across the street. He also noted the direction from which Francome was coming.

'He's been to see the whore!' Cleve said to himself. 'Now has he been indulgin' in some dangerous pillow talk? Guess I need to find that out afore I kill him.'

It was close on midnight when Angie knocked at the door of Nat's hotel room. The desk clerk had raised an eyebrow when she'd told him she was paying Nat visit, and checked his room number.

'Not *that* kind of visit, Barney,' she had told him.

'It's just that it's kinda late,' he'd said.

'Then let's hope Mr Leach is a light sleeper.'

As it happened, Nat had not yet gone to bed. He'd been sitting in the room's one and only chair cogitating on the night's events and had finally dozed off, only to be woken by Angie's knocking. It being an unusual time to be receiving visitors, Nat picked up his .45 before cautiously opening the door.

'Angie!' He smiled. 'Well, this is a pleasant surprise, but . . .'

Angie brushed past him into the room. 'You're as bad as the desk clerk, jumping to conclusions,' she said. 'I'm here with some information.'

Nat put his gun on the washstand and indicated to Angie to take the chair. He perched on the edge of the bed. 'Must be important if it can't wait until morning,' he said.

'That's for you to decide, but I reckoned you should hear it as soon as possible,' Angie said, and went on to relate her conversation with Ches Francome.

'So Francome is *definitely* Travis Newton,' Nat said.

'And Cleve Connor – real name Jess Taggart – is the fourth man you're looking for,' Angie said. 'What's more, he could also be Jacob Hawley.'

'And Joe Spearing's killer.' Nat rose from the bed and began strapping on his gunbelt. 'Time I paid our good sheriff another visit.'

'What, now?' Angie said. 'He's probably drinking himself into a stupor.'

'Or he could be heading out of town to warn Connor. I plan to see him before he gets a chance to do that.'

Angie shook her head. 'He won't do that. He thinks what he told me will stay with me, and anyway he's too scared of Connor to admit blabbing.'

'Even so, I'm going to make sure.'

'So he's going to know I've told on him,' Angie said. She shrugged. 'Oh well, it had to be done. But I reckon I'll lay low for a day or two, until all this is resolved one way or another.'

'Thanks, Angie.' He put an arm round her shoulders and hugged her. 'I owe you more than I can say.'

'Just don't get yourself killed, Nat. Connor's a dangerous man.'

Nat grinned. 'So am I.'

There were still people coming from the saloon as Nat walked along the main street. As he drew near to the sheriff's office, he could see a dim glow of lamplight coming from the window. And he could see two shadows inside. Next came a dull, muted *phut!*, which to Nat sounded like a muffled gunshot. This was immediately confirmed as one of the two shadows fell and the other moved quickly away.

Nat glanced around, but nobody but himself was near enough to the sheriff's office to have heard the noise. He quickened his pace and pushed the office door open. Francome's body lay in an ungainly heap beside his desk.

A sound from the back indicated that the killer was still in the building. Nat drew his gun and made for the door to Francome's private quarters. It was in darkness, but he saw a retreating shadow open the back door and step out into the night. Nat took two strides, loosing off a shot. But in the darkness in the room he didn't see the small table beside the bed, and stumbled into it. His shot missed its target as he fell headlong over it, and the unidentified killer made his getaway.

Nat swore.

After getting to his feet, he went back into the office to see if there was anything he could do for Francome, but a quick check for a pulse established that the sheriff was beyond help.

It was as he was getting up from his knees that he became aware of two or three others crowding in the doorway. He also became aware that he was still holding his six-shooter and that the newcomers were eyeing it with alarm. He re-holstered the weapon.

'Francome's dead. Shot,' he said. 'The killer got away. I fired a shot to stop him, but I tripped and missed.' He wasn't sure why he felt such an urgent need to explain.

Maybe it was the suspicious looks on the men's faces.

'We only heard the one shot,' one of them said. Nat recognized him as Ted Brewster from the saddle shop. 'That's what brought us running.'

'The killer muffled his shot,' Nat said. He looked around to see if he could locate anything that might have been used to suppress the noise, but there was nothing obvious. Whatever he had used, the killer had taken it with him. 'The shot you heard was mine, like I just explained.'

At that moment, Chap Fancy pushed his way through the huddle in the doorway. When he saw Francome, he let out an oath, then stared at Nat.

'What happened here, Leach?' he said.

Nat explained, constantly aware of the sceptical expressions on the faces around him.

'What brought you here?' Chap said. 'It's damn late to be payin' a visit 'lessen you've got somethin' mighty important to discuss. Care to tell me what that was?'

'Yes, I'll tell you,' Nat said. 'But maybe we could have a little privacy.'

Chap nodded. 'OK, but I'll take your gun.'

Nat eased the weapon from his holster and handed it over. Chap sniffed the barrel.

'Been fired,' he confirmed.

'Like I told you, I fired a shot after the killer.'

'We only heard the one shot, Chap,' Ted Brewster said.

'Yeah, OK, Ted,' Chap said. 'Leach here had an explanation for that.'

'Yeah, the muffled gun. And you believe it?'

'I don't know what I believe right now,' Chap said. 'But I'd be obliged if you an' the others would make yourselves scarce, so that I can hear the reasons Leach had for comin' here. Meantime, one of you go an' get Jasper Harrison to take Ches's body away.'

Reluctantly, the onlookers dispersed and Chap closed the door after them. He sat himself down in Francome's chair and indicated to Nat to take the one opposite.

'Start talkin',' he said.

Nat sighed and began his tale. As the minutes passed, he watched Chap's expression darken as he listened to Nat's recounting of his meeting with Angie and what she had told him about the sheriff.

'So you planned to accuse Ches of bein' this Travis Newton *hombre*, and accuse him of rapin' and killin' your mother an' sister?' Chap said when Nat had finished.

'Him and Cleve Connor,' Nat said.

Chap stroked the stubble on his chin. 'An' what d'you plan to do now?'

'Confront Connor,' Nat said. 'I reckon he must be most of the way back to the Circle C by now – *after killing Francome*.'

'You sayin' it was Connor you saw retreatin' out of the back door an' shot at?' Chap said.

'I can't be certain, but I'd lay odds on it. From what Angie told me, Francome had a loose mouth, so Connor would be anxious to close it – permanently.'

Chap took a wad of tobacco from his vest pocket and put it in his mouth. He chewed silently for several moments, then said, 'You see my difficulty, don't you, Leach? I've only got your word as to what happened. Ted Brewster an' the others swear they only heard one shot, an' when I arrived earlier you were standing over Ches's body with a gun that had been fired.'

'So what are you going to do?' Nat asked.

'Well, for one thing, I ain't goin' to let you high-tail it to the Circle C and put a bullet in Cleve Connor,' Chap said. 'Maybe he is this "fourth man" you talk about, but maybe he isn't. And the thing is, in your present state of mind you're more'n likely to shoot first an' ask questions afterwards.'

'So?' Nat asked.

Chap eased Nat's six-gun that he was holding into a position whereby it was pointing directly at its owner. 'Reckon I'll let you cool down in one of my cells until mornin' an' I've had time to think some more. Now I'm hopin' you're gonna be reasonable an' not give me any trouble, 'cause Ches Francome, for all his faults, was a good friend of mine.'

'Some friend,' Nat said. 'A rapist and a murderer.'

'So you say,' Chap said. 'But I think I need to hear Cleve's side of the story afore I start accusin' him of anythin'. Little late to go visitin' now, so I guess it'll have to wait until mornin'.' He rose out of the chair, keeping the gun level and pointing it at Nat's midriff. With his other hand, he took a bunch of keys from a drawer.

At that moment, the door opened and Jasper Harrison came in. For a split second, Nat thought about using the distraction to upend the desk and take his gun back, but he decided against it. It would only strengthen folks' suspicions of his guilt if he went against the town's remaining lawman. For the moment he would bide his time.

The undertaker had frozen in the doorway, taking in the scene.

127

'It's all right, Jasper,' Chap said. 'Mr Leach was just goin' to accompany me to the cells where he'll be spendin' the night. You carry on with your business.'

CHAPTER 18

Unlike Francome, Chap wasn't nervous when talking to Cleve Connor in the normal run of things. But when it came to accusing him of murdering the sheriff, the words stuck in Chap's craw as he stood in front of Connor's desk.

Connor seemed to sense this. 'Spit it out, Chap,' he said. 'What's on your mind? Guess it must be important if it brings you to the Circle C this early in the morning.'

'Yes, well, first off let me say I don't necessarily believe what Leach is sayin', but I wouldn't be doin' my job if I didn't . . .'

'Leach?' Connor said. 'What's he got to do with anythin'? And if it's so important, why isn't Ches here to explain? It's not that I don't trust you, Chap, but Ches is sheriff, after all.'

'Not any more he ain't,' Chap said. 'Ches got himself shot last night. Killed in his own office.'

'What!' Connor exploded. 'Why? Who killed him? What in hell happened?'

'Well, that's what I was about to explain.'

'You mentioned the Leach fellah,' Connor said. 'Was it

him who shot Ches?' He slammed a fist down on his desk top. 'I knew that bastard was dangerous!'

'Hold fire a second, Cleve,' Chap said. 'Thing is, he's accusin' *you* of bein' the shootist.'

'*What!*'

'An' that's not all he's accusin' you of.' Chap swallowed and mopped his forehead with his neckerchief. 'Mind if I sit down, Cleve?'

Connor nodded to the chair opposite him. 'Go ahead. Guess you might as well be comfortable if you're going to tell me some fairy story.'

Once seated, Chap took a deep breath and began. 'First off, Leach says your name ain't Cleve Connor, it's Jess Taggart. Furthermore, he says you an' three other men an' killed his mother an' sister, an' that it happened during the War. He – he reckons the four of you were deserters.'

'That's a damn lie!' Connor shouted. 'All of it's a lie!'

'He says Ches's real name was Travis Newton, an' that you killed him because you were afraid Ches would blab about the whole thing – somethin' he did, as it happens. To Angie Smith, who told Leach.'

'The whore? You and Leach would take the word of a *whore?*'

'Seems Leach had figured out most of it before she confirmed it, all 'ceptin' your real name,' Ches said. 'Anyways, he was on his way to tackle Ches about it last night when he heard a muffled shot come from the office. By the time he got there, Ches was lyin' dead on the floor. But Leach heard somebody leave through the back door. He ran out and fired a shot after the critter, but missed.'

'Any witnesses to this so-called muffled shot, except Leach?'

Chap shook his head. 'Folks only heard the one shot – the one Leach swears he fired at the killer.'

'So there you have it. Leach is lying. He killed Ches.'

'But why would he? Unless the story about his ma an' sister is true, an' Ches was Travis Newton, an' Leach was avengin' their murders. In which case, you . . .'

'*In which case nothin'!*' Connor slammed his fist down a second time. 'If Leach's story about his mother and sister is true – and personally I don't believe a word of it – it has nothin' to do with me. Ches and some other men, maybe. But not me.'

'So why would Ches tell Angie Smith you were part of it?'

'Who knows what stories Francome would make up when he was drunk? Fact is, he knew I was thinkin' it was time we had a more reliable sheriff, one who didn't drink himself into a stupor most days. Maybe he mentioned my name out of spite.'

'I – I guess that's possible,' Chap said, doubtfully.

'Believe it,' Connor said. 'You've got your killer, Chap. Just make sure he hangs.'

Lyle Walker drew his buggy to a halt a half mile short of the Circle C. He saw the figure of the deputy sheriff leaving the ranch house, and decided it might be better if he didn't meet up with him, considering the reason he had for visiting with Cleve Connor. Best if that was kept confidential.

Instead of continuing his journey on to the ranch

house, he headed towards a stand of trees where he could wait concealed until after the deputy was well past.

As he waited, he pondered over the possible reason Chap Fancy could have had for calling on Connor. Could it have anything to do with the killing of Chesney Francome? News of the sheriff's murder had spread quickly that morning, and Lyle had been both shocked and curious about the reasons behind it. Word was that Nat Leach was being held for the killing, but it was unclear why the newcomer should want to kill Francome.

Lyle wondered if it was connected in any way with the reason for his visit to Connor, but he couldn't see how.

Unless. . . .

Gabe listened to the account Angie gave of Ches Francome's visit to her the previous night, and all that the now-dead sheriff had admitted. They were sitting in Angie's private parlour, a pot of coffee on the table between them.

'Pretty much what we and Nat suspected,' he said when she had finished. 'And Nat left here to go and confront Francome?'

'That's right,' Angie said.

'And got himself accused of his murder,' Gabe said, slowly shaking his head. 'Crazy.'

'You . . . you don't think Nat. . . ?' Angie began.

'*Did* kill Francome? No, I don't.'

'He was all-fired angry when he left here,' Angie said. She poured fresh coffee into their cups. 'And he did say he'd kill the two remaining murderers of his ma and sister when he found them.'

132

'Even so, he wouldn't come up with some story about the killer leaving through the back door and firing a shot after him. If he had killed Francome he would have admitted it and given his reason for doing so.'

Angie nodded. 'Yes, I guess he would at that.'

'So the best guess is that Cleve Connor killed Francome and managed to dodge Nat's bullet. But we can't prove it.' He drained his coffee cup and stood up. 'First thing to do is get Nat out of jail.'

'How are you going to do that?' Angie said.

'By trying to talk some sense into Chap Fancy.'

Nat sat on the edge of the cot in the corner of his prison cell. He'd had very little sleep, his mind too occupied with all that he'd learned. He'd tried to think of a way of legally bringing Cleve Connor – now known to be Jess Taggart – to justice for the murders of his mother and sister, but had failed to come up with one. For a start, how could he prove what he was certain to be true? Now all the three others responsible were dead and he only had Francome's word-of-mouth evidence, via Angie, that Connor was the fourth man. Not good enough to convince a judge. Connor simply had to deny everything.

Nat sighed. So, retribution was down to him and him alone. Well, he'd always suspected it would be.

He heard the outer door of the office open and close. Moments later, Chap Fancy came through to the cells. He'd obviously stopped off at Freda's eating house and collected ham and eggs for Nat's breakfast.

'I'm gonna open the cell door to hand this over,' Chap said. 'Just don't try anythin' stupid 'cause I'll have my

133

other hand on my six-gun.'

'It's OK, Chap,' Nat said. 'If you remember, I'm not armed. Besides, I'm mighty hungry and that ham smells good.'

Chap fetched a mug of coffee and passed it through the cell bars.

'I've been to see Cleve Connor,' he told Nat.

'Guessed you had,' Nat said, through a mouthful of ham.

'Seems like it's your word against his,' Chap said.

Nat nodded and swigged his coffee. 'Guessed it would be. So what now?'

Before the deputy could answer, they heard somebody come into the office, and Chap went to see who it was.

He sighed. 'Mornin', Gabe,' he said. 'Guessed it wouldn't be long afore you made an appearance. What can I do for you?'

'You can open that cage and let an innocent man go free, Chap,' Gabe said. 'Leach didn't kill Ches. Oh, sure, he had reason enough to kill him, but he wouldn't have done it without confronting him first with what he knew about Ches being Travis Newton and Connor being Jess Taggart.'

'We don't know Connor is Taggart,' Chap began.

'Yet from what I can gather,' Gabe went on, as if the other man hadn't spoken, 'Nat had left the hotel just minutes before your so-called witnesses heard the shot, which they claim was the one that killed Ches. Barely enough time for Nat to make it to this office, let alone enter into a conversation with the sheriff before killing him. No, Nat's explanation makes the most sense. The shot your witnesses heard was the one Nat fired after the departing killer. In all probability, Cleve Connor.'

Chap glanced back towards the cells. Uncertainty was written all over his face. 'I can't just let Leach loose for him to go an' take a shot at Connor,' he said.

'Even if Connor – Taggart – deserves it?' Gabe said. 'Well, OK, I see what you're saying. We need to get proof that he was involved in the murder of Nat's sister and mother.'

'How you gonna do that?' Chap wanted to know. 'From what I've heard, it all happened during the War. That's years ago.'

'Listen, let me talk to Nat. Then if I guarantee he won't do anything rash until we've at least had a chance to see what we can find out about Connor's war record, will you let him out?'

'You want me to free him on *your word*, Gabe?'

Gabe nodded. 'It'll be his word, too. And I believe Nat Leach is a man of his word.'

'OK,' Chap said. 'But I'm sure gonna have to do a lot of explainin' to folks, especially Cleve Connor, when they see Leach walkin' the streets.'

'Leave Connor to me,' Gabe said. 'I'll have words with him. Now, are you going to let me talk with Nat?'

'All right,' Chap said. 'But, if I let him go an' he agrees to what you're suggestin', I'm makin' you responsible for him.'

'Sure, sure,' Gabe said impatiently.

Twenty minutes later Nat had gathered up his belongings, including his gun, and he and Gabe were walking to the newspaper office.

CHAPTER 19

'Seems like your morning for visitors, Cleve,' Lyle Walker said as he followed the rancher to the latter's study.

'Mm? What?' A disconcerted Connor was wondering what Walker had on his mind. As far as he could remember, this was the first time the would-be mayor had come to the Circle C.

'I saw Chap Fancy leave here earlier,' Lyle explained. 'Did he come to tell you about Ches Francome's murder?'

The two men found seats in the study, Cleve in the swivel chair behind his desk and Lyle on the leather couch under the window.

'Yeah,' Cleve said. 'He did. Got that Leach fellah in a cell after folks heard the gunshot and found the critter beside Ches's body. Guess he'll hang for it. Whatever, we'll be needin' a new sheriff. Chap Fancy's too old for the job. Any suggestions, Lyle?'

'Can't say I have,' Lyle said.

'No, well, I guess it'll need some thought.' Cleve was

silent for a moment or two, then he said, 'Anyway, what can I do for you, Lyle?'

'You can make sure I get enough votes to ensure I'm elected mayor,' Lyle said, looking directly at the other man.

Cleve raised his eyebrows and didn't speak for a full half minute. When he did, it was to say, 'What makes you think I can do that, Lyle?'

Lyle smiled. 'We both know the amount of – what shall I say? – *influence* you have over a number of voters. A word or two from you and they'll fall into line, isn't that right?'

Cleve looked amused. 'Let's just assume what you're saying is correct, but why would I support you rather than Howard Ellis?'

Lyle looked out of the study window, as if surveying the extent of Cleve Connor's territory. 'Because I know something Howard doesn't . . . Jess?' And he turned in time to see the blood drain from Cleve's face.

'Who. . . ?'

'Ches Francome,' Lyle said. 'Some months ago. Of course he was drunk at the time, otherwise I guess he wouldn't have let it slip. We had this card school on a Friday night at my house – myself, Ted Brewster, Otis Bream and Ches. I always enjoy a game of poker, providing the stakes aren't too high. Learned my lesson about that some years ago. Anyway, one night Ches had drunk more than his usual intake of brandy so I decided it would be sensible to walk him back to his office. He was grateful and began to get maudlin, saying how few friends he had in Ox Crossing apart from those he'd spent the evening with and . . . *Jess*. Of couse, I said

"Who's Jess?" and without thinking he replied, "Cleve. Good old Cleve!" Well, to cut a long story short, I probed a bit and he came up with your full name – Jess Taggart.'

Cleve stared at him without speaking. Somehow it seemed pointless to deny it. The question was, how much more did Walker know? Clearly what Chap Fancy had discovered hadn't spread – yet – and Cleve had planned to deny it all if and when it did. After all, without proof he was safe, and with luck and Leach hanged for the murder of Ches Francome, eventually the story would die a natural death. But if the well respected Lyle Walker was to be allowed to add what *he'd* learned into the mix of the stories going round . . .

He waited for several moments, then said, 'That it?'

Lyle shrugged. 'Well, I guess there's more, otherwise you wouldn't be using a false name, Cleve, but Ches clammed up once he realized he'd said too much. Still, I reckon whatever you're keeping quiet about will soon surface if I spread the word about your real name. Somebody like Gabe Crighton might take it into his head to start digging into your past, too, just to see if there was a story for his newspaper.'

'And do you plan to do that? "Spread the word"? No, let me guess. You'll keep this titbit of information to yourself if I vote for you for mayor.'

'And let other folks know that's what you're going to do,' Lyle said. 'You've got it.'

Cleve gave a mirthless laugh. 'Well, I guess you'll make as good a mayor as Howard Ellis.'

'Better,' Lyle said.

And you'll use what Francome told you about me every time you want my support for something. I'll be your whipping boy, Lyle, forever at your mercy.

Cleve felt the anger burning inside him, but he forced himself to appear calm. 'OK, we have a deal,' he said.

'As to why you're living under a false name,' Lyle said, adopting an avuncular tone, 'I don't want to know. It's not important. We all have our secrets, after all.'

You'll find out soon enough when you get back to town.

'True,' Cleve said. 'What's your secret, Lyle?'

The other man laughed and stood up. 'I'll be seeing you, Cleve,' he said. And he turned and walked out of the room.

'You know what, Lyle?' Cleve muttered to himself when he was alone. 'You just signed your own death warrant.'

When Gabe and Nat arrived at the newspaper office, Toby greeted them with a surprised look on his face.

'They let you out?' he said to Nat.

Nat grinned. 'Thanks to some fancy talking by Gabe.'

'Listen,' Gabe said to Toby. 'Nat can give you the details about what we've learned, then you can start drafting a report.'

'Are you planning to put it all in?' Nat asked. 'Who Francome was? Connor's real name? What they and the other two did?'

'We can't mention Connor specifically,' Gabe said. 'Have to watch the libel angle. After all, most of it's hearsay, without real evidence or proof. But it'll set a fire under Connor, and then we'll see what happens.'

'What are you going to do?' Toby asked.

139

'I'm going to the telegraph office,' Gabe said. 'I reckon there should be a reply to my wire by now.'

'From your editor friend in Stokewood?' Toby said.

'That's it. I'll see you both a bit later.'

After Gabe was gone, Nat recounted to Toby what he had learned from Angie Smith, including the real identities of Sheriff Francome and Cleve Connor and what they and the two other men had done to Nat's family during the War.

Toby scribbled notes on a pad.

When he had finished, Nat said, 'Let's hope Gabe hears something useful from Stokewood, then we can think about Joe Spearing's killing as well. To be honest, that's my first priority. Getting Joe's killer, or the man who ordered his murder.'

Toby hesitated before saying, 'Matter of fact, Molly made mention of Stokewood.'

'She did?' Nat was suddenly interested.

'Yes. She heard her stepfather talking with her mother, and was sure she heard the name Stokewood mentioned. Anyway, she asked her ma about it.'

'What did her mother say?'

'Apparently she got quite angry and denied ever having the conversation between herself and her husband, about Stokewood or whether he knew anybody there.'

'But Molly was sure the conversation took place?'

'Yes. It was a few months ago. Probably around the time Joey Spearing was killed. So . . .'

'Hang on, what did you just say?' Nat said quickly.

'I said it was about the time Joe Spearing was murdered.'

Nat shook his head. 'No, you didn't. You said *Joey* Spearing.'

'Did I? Well it must have been how Molly referred to him. Anyway, she got real angry with me. Accusing me of implying that her mother and stepfather had something to do with Joe Spearing's murder.'

'But she definitely said *Joey* and not Joe? You're sure?'

Toby thought for a moment, then nodded. 'I'm sure. Why is it important?'

'Because Joe never used the name Joey after he left Stokewood, I'm certain. He would get quite annoyed if anyone called him by that name. Said it was a kid's name, and he was no kid any more.'

'So . . . what are you saying? That it suggests Kyle or Jane Walker knew Joe Spearing when he was a kid, before he came to Ox Crossing?'

'Maybe. Which means that at one time one or both of them must have lived or passed through Stokewood,' Nat said.

'Not Mrs Walker,' Toby said. 'She's lived here in Ox Crossing since before Molly was born, when she was Mrs Brownlow.'

'So it must have been Kyle Walker,' said Nat.

'Which means he might have known Jabal Hawley, and would know who he is now that he's living in Ox Crossing.'

Nat looked thoughtful. 'Yes, it's possible. I think I should go and have a chat with the Walker family.'

'Oh, heck! Now Molly'll be even madder at me for mentioning her conversation with her mother to you.'

'Don't worry, I'll try not to bring that into it,' Nat said.

Though he had a feeling he was going to have to go back on his word.

Nora Millington passed Bud Weston's wire to Gabe, a quizzical look in her eye. She was a tall woman with her iron grey hair pulled back into a bun.

'It's a long one,' she said. 'Must've cost your friend a packet. I hope it's worth it, Gabe.'

'I think it might be,' Gabe said. 'Thanks, Nora. You OK?'

'Well, I'd be lying if I said I wasn't feeling a bit nervous after what happened to Mr Jarvis,' she replied. 'But I like the job fine. Needed something to keep me occupied after Kit died.'

'He was a fine man, your husband,' Gabe said. 'Should've been him running for mayor. Reckon he'd have got the job.'

Nora shook her head. 'Kit was no friend of Cleve Connor, and it'll be him who'll sway the votes.'

'Guess you're right,' Gabe admitted.

Instead of going back to the newspaper office immediately, Gabe took the wire to the saloon where he ordered a beer and found a quiet table to absorb the contents of the telegraph without distractions.

By the time he had finished reading what Bud Weston had to say, his beer remained untouched and his head was spinning with new possibilities. He stared ahead of him trying to make sense of what he had learned. If what Bud was hinting at was right, then he and Nat and Angie had been looking at the mystery of the identity of the man Joe Spearing had seen from the wrong angle.

Twenty minutes later he walked back into the newspaper office. Toby was working on the report for the newspaper. The young man looked up.

'Your friend's reply arrive?' Toby asked.

'It did,' Gabe said. 'Nat not here?'

'Nope,' Toby said. 'He's gone to see Lyle Walker.'

'What for?' Gabe said quickly.

'It was something Mrs Walker said about Joe Spearing,' Toby said.

'What about him?'

Toby frowned. 'What's up, Gabe? You sound worried.'

'Just tell me what Jane Walker said that's sent Nat off to see Lyle Walker,' Gabe said. 'It could be important.'

'Well, it seems possible Mr Walker may have lived in Stokewood sometime before the War,' Toby said, and went on to recount what Molly had told him, and the conclusions Nat had come to.

Gabe listened with what seemed to be a mounting alarm. When Toby had finished he nodded slowly to himself.

'Makes sense,' he said.

'What does?' Toby asked.

'Tell you later,' Gabe said. And he hurried from the office.

Toby carried on writing for another fifteen minutes, but he found it hard to concentrate. If things were going to turn nasty at the Walker residence, he wanted to be there to support Molly.

He checked the clock on the wall. She would be finishing at the school in another half hour. Maybe he would go and meet her. Escort her home. It would also be an opportunity to try and smooth things over between them.

Yes, he'd do that.

CHAPTER 20

'My husband's not home right now, Mr Leach,' Jane Walker said.

'When do you expect him back?' Nat smiled to take the edge off the abruptness of his question.

'I'm not sure. He didn't say.'

They were standing in the front porch of the Walker residence and Nat could feel the heat of the sun on his back. 'I wonder if I could take up a few minutes of your time, Mrs Walker,' he said.

'Well . . . I don't see how I can be . . .'

'Just a few minutes,' Nat cut in. 'It's kinda important.'

'Oh, very well.' She stepped back to allow him to pass inside the house. 'Come through to the parlour.'

'Parlour' seemed an inadequate word for the impressive large room she led him into. The furnishings spoke of wealth combined with good taste, almost certainly selected by Jane Walker, Nat judged. He wondered how much of it had been acquired when she had been married to her first husband. French doors overlooked a stretch of grass and large shrubs at the back of the house.

Jane Walker sat down on the edge of a high-backed chair and indicated for Nat to do the same. It was a gesture designed to imply that he shouldn't make himself too comfortable.

'So, how can I help you?' she said, smoothing down the front of her dress and placing her hands in her lap.

Nat saw no merit in beating about the bush. 'When were you or your husband in Stokewood?' he asked. And watched the colour spread across her cheeks.

'I've never been to Stokewood,' she said after a moment.

'And your husband?'

She waited several seconds before asking, 'What is this all about, Mr Leach?'

'It's about the death – the murder – of a good friend of mine, Mrs Walker. Joe Spearing.' Nat held her gaze. 'Or perhaps you knew him better as *Joey* Spearing.'

'I didn't know him at all,' Jane Walker replied quickly. Too quickly, Nat thought.

'But he came here, to your house, at least once,' Nat said.

'If he did, it was to see my husband.' She was looking increasingly uncomfortable.

Nat nodded slowly. 'I guess that's it. He came to see Mr Walker – *who knew him well enough to call him "Joey"*. A name Joe Spearing hadn't used since he was a kid. How do you explain that? Unless your husband knew him *when* he was a kid?'

'She doesn't need to explain anything, Leach. Not to you.' The voice came from behind Nat, and he turned quickly to see Lyle Walker standing in the doorway, a thunderous expression on his face. 'Who the hell do you think you are, upsetting my wife with your questions?' He walked into the room and faced Nat.

'Forgive me, Mr Walker,' Nat said easily, getting up from his seat. 'It wasn't my intention to upset anyone. I was just trying to clear something up. Maybe you can help.'

'I don't feel inclined to help you in any shape or form, Leach,' Lyle Walker said. 'Now, I'd be obliged if you'd leave.'

'Then maybe you'd be prepared to help *me* out, Lyle?' The voice came from the hallway this time, followed swiftly by the appearance of Gabe Crighton in the doorway.

'What the. . .!' Lyle began.

'Sorry to intrude, Lyle, but the porch door was open and I heard voices. Guessed it was prudent to come and join the party before tempers got too frayed.' Gabe smiled sweetly at Jane Walker. 'Howdy, Jane, you're looking as lovely as ever.'

'Listen, Gabe,' Lyle said, struggling to remain calm. 'If you know what this is all about, I'd be obliged if you'd explain.'

'Why don't we all sit down and try to sort out this – uh – problem,' Gabe said, moving to a leather chair and easing himself down on to it.

'There is no problem,' Lyle said. He crossed the room and stood, legs apart, fists clenched by his side, with his back to the French doors. 'Other than the fact that Leach comes blustering in here intimidating Jane with his questions.'

'Intimidating?' Gabe said. 'Dear, dear, I hope that's not

147

true, Nat. No, I'm sure it's not.' He settled himself more comfortably before going on. 'The thing is, Lyle, as Nat was saying, you seem to have known the name people called Joe Spearing when he was a kid. A name he never used after he left Stokewood to join the Confederacy. Which, I grant you, means very little on its own.'

'Exactly!' Lyle said, exasperation showing all over his face. 'I may have called the man "Joey", but if I did it was probably a friendly gesture, nothing more. People sometimes call Jane "Janey", it doesn't mean anything.'

Gabe nodded. 'Like I said, on its own it doesn't amount to much.'

'But?' Nat put in, suddenly sensing more.

'I have an old friend,' Gabe explained. 'He's in the same business as me, editing a small town newspaper. A long time ago we were both reporters on the same newspaper in Phoenix and we've kept in touch over the years.'

'What's all this got to do with me?' Lyle said, obviously irritated.

'My friend's name is Bud Weston,' Gabe said. 'He's editor of the *Stokewood Times*. Maybe you knew him at one time, Lyle. He's worked for the paper since before the War.'

'How would I? I've never been to Stokewood as far as I can remember.'

'I sent him a wire, a while ago,' Gabe went on, as if the other man hadn't spoken. 'Got a reply, too, although I never saw it. Know why that was? Because Cliff Jarvis intercepted it and used it to try and blackmail someone. And took a bullet for his pains. Anyway, I sent a second wire to Bud and this time – an hour ago – I received a reply.'

He paused and looked at Jane Walker, then Lyle.

'What's it got to do with us, Gabe?' Jane asked, her face pale. 'What did your friend have to say that concerns Lyle and me?'

'He was answering some questions I posed about an eleven-year-old crime in Stokewood,' Gabe said. 'And a man called Jabal Hawley.'

'The man Toby Greenway wrote about in your paper?' Jane asked.

Gabe nodded. 'Although Bud's reply was more about the man whom Hawley supposedly killed. A man called Martin Benson.'

'*Supposedly* killed?' Nat said. 'Are you saying somebody else might've killed Benson?'

Gabe took a deep breath before answering. 'No, I'm saying *Martin Benson killed Jabal Hawley*. I'm saying the person your friend Joe saw here in Ox Crossing back in February was *Martin Benson*.'

'Jeeze!' Nat said. 'But the body in the real estate office. . . ?'

'The remains of the body after the fire,' Gabe corrected, 'were identified by two things, according to Bud, who actually wrote the report for the *Stokewood Times*. A pocket watch, engraved with the initials "MB", and a very distinctive ring which Benson was known to wear. Both of which Benson could have planted on Hawley if he wanted everyone to believe that he, Benson, was the victim.'

'And Bud Weston reckons this is what happened?' Nat said. 'Benson killed Hawley and then disappeared?'

'Bud says he's had his suspicions for years, but has never voiced them because there was no way of proving anything.'

'This is all very interesting, I'm sure,' Lyle said. 'But what has it got to do with Jane and I? Really, Gabe, it might make an interesting theory to use as the basis for some newspaper article, but it's all conjecture.'

'Did Benson have a reason for wanting to disappear?' Nat asked.

'Several,' Gabe replied. 'He had heavy gambling debts.' He looked at Lyle. 'Like you, Lyle, he liked his game of poker and was part of a regular card school. Also, it was well known by townsfolk that he had come to hate both his wife and his job. He made no secret of either. His father-in-law was his employer, by the way. An influential bully, according to Bud.'

'So you're saying this Benson *hombre* is still alive?' Nat said.

'I'm pretty sure he is,' Gabe said. 'His wife certainly is. So if he *is* alive and he's married again, he's a bigamist.'

A small gasp came from Jane Walker.

'Did you want to say something, Jane?' Gabe asked.

She shook her head. 'No, nothing. As Lyle said, this has nothing to do with us.'

Gabe turned to her husband. 'That right, Lyle?'

'Of course it's right!' the other man snapped.

'Hold on, Gabe,' Nat put in. 'Are you saying . . . *Mr Walker* here is Martin Benson?'

'Are you, Lyle?' Gabe asked.

'No! Damned if I am!' Lyle shouted.

Gabe took a sheet of paper from the pocket of his jacket and unfolded it. It was one of the election flyers encouraging folks to vote for Lyle Walker. There was also a picture of Lyle dead centre.

'So if I was to send a handful of these to Bud to distribute around Stokewood,' he said, 'nobody would claim this was the picture of a supposedly dead man, Martin Benson – is that right, Lyle? Eleven years isn't a long time. Folks remember. And if Joe Spearing recognized you, in spite of that handsome moustache of yours, I reckon they would, too.'

Lyle said nothing for some minutes. All the while his wife stared at him in mute horror. Eventually, he turned and looked out of the window, his back to the others.

Nat and Gabe exchanged glances.

'You going to do that, Gabe?' Lyle said at last. 'Send some of the flyers to Stokewood?'

'No need to if you come clean, Lyle,' Gabe said.

'And admit you're Benson and that you killed – or arranged the killing of – Joe Spearing when you found out he'd recognized you,' Nat added.

'Well, Lyle?' Gabe said. 'What's it to be?'

Jane began to sob.

Lyle stared at Gabe for several seconds, then he turned and looked across at his wife. 'I'm sorry, my dear, I should have . . .'

The sudden explosion came as the glass in one of the French doors shattered and Lyle Walker pitched forward with part of his head blown away.

Jane Walker screamed as Gabe cursed and Nat threw himself on to the floor amongst the glass splinters, drawing his six-gun at the same time. A bullet whistled over his head and smashed a glass vase over the fireplace.

'Shots are coming from the shrubbery!' he yelled at Gabe, and fired a shot in that direction. 'I saw the flash!'

'Rifle shot,' Gabe agreed. 'Winchester, probably.'

Nat fired a second shot into the shrubbery, and moments later, a figure in a long grey duster zig-zagged across the grass and out through a gate that led into a back street. His Stetson was pulled low and his face was half covered by a neckerchief. He was carrying a Winchester.

Nat loosed off three more shots, but none found their target.

'Who in hell. . . ?' Gabe said.

Nat didn't wait to reply. He pushed his way through the wrecked glass doors and went in pursuit of the killer.

Jane Walker started to move towards her dead husband. Gabe took hold of her gently and guided her into one of the large easy chairs. She was shaking uncontrollably, a whimpering noise coming from her mouth.

'How much of this did you know, Jane?' Gabe asked gently.

She sighed. 'Joe Spearing came to see Lyle and I heard bits of their conversation. Lyle called him Joey, but I thought nothing of that. I heard the name Jabal Hawley mentioned, and the town of Stokewood. I spoke to Lyle afterwards, but he told me to forget what I'd overheard, that it wasn't important. I believed him.' She shook her head. 'No, I guess I *wanted* to believe him.'

'And when Joe Spearing was killed? Didn't that make you—?'

'I just refused to believe Lyle had anything to do with it,' Jane cut in.

'And now?' Gabe prompted.

She shrugged. 'It seems Lyle was about to explain,

but . . .' She looked down at her husband's lifeless form. 'Who?' she asked, her voice little more than a whisper. 'Who would do. . . ?'

Gabe sighed. He had his suspicions about 'who'. Something about the escaping killer was familiar in spite of the obvious attempt at disguise. And the fact that the *hombre* found it *necessary* to conceal his identity suggested that, if he hadn't, he would have been easily recognizable.

Molly Brownlow was making her way home from the schoolhouse, a wide-brimmed straw hat shielding her face from the early afternoon sunshine. She had enjoyed another morning with the children, but there was a heaviness in her heart whenever she thought about Toby.

Had she been too quick to accuse him of suspecting her parents of covering up something bad about the murder of Joe Spearing? *Joey* Spearing. Her mother *had* called him by that name, she was certain. It wasn't something she'd made up. But what did it all mean?

Molly was convinced her mother knew nothing about the killing, but her stepfather. . . ? What did she and her ma really know about Lyle Walker? He had come into their lives after the War, and within a few short months had swept Jane Brownlow off her feet and married her. But what did they know about his past?

The road from the school passed the back of Molly's home, and as she drew nearer to the wooden gate that led into the back of the property, the gate flew open and the figure of a man burst out and started running in her direction. He wore a long duster and he was clutching a rifle in one hand. As he ran, he lost his Stetson and the neckerchief covering part of his face slipped down.

'Mr Connor!'

Molly recognized Cleve Connor at the same moment that Connor realized his mask had slipped and that the stepdaughter of the man he'd just killed had identified him.

'*Shee-it!*' Connor muttered. Then, to make things worse, he heard the gate slam shut behind him and the feet of his pursuer.

Molly stopped in her tracks but Connor kept running until he was alongside her.

'Wh . . . what's happened, Mr Connor?' she cried, then took in the expression on his face and immediately sensed something was terribly wrong, and that she was in some kind of danger because of it.

Then she saw the Leach man, and where he'd come from. He was clutching a gun, and he must have heard how Molly addressed the man with the Winchester.

'Hold it, *Taggart!*' Nat yelled.

Connor grabbed Molly's arm and dragged her back in the direction from which she'd come. 'Reckon I might need some insurance, missy,' he said. 'An' you're it.'

Molly screamed and tried to resist but his grip was too strong.

'You can't get away, Taggart.' Nat levelled his six-gun, pointing it at the retreating pair. 'I have got the name right, haven't I? You're the fourth murdering bastard, the man I've been looking for, aren't you?'

Cleve pulled Molly in front of him to act as a shield, one arm wrapped across her breasts. Then he shoved the barrel of the Winchester against the back of her head.

154

'What if I am?' he yelled. 'Drop it! Drop the gun, or missy here will be dead meat.'

Nat hesitated for a second, then dropped his weapon.

'What're you planning on doing, Taggart?' he asked. 'You've no place to go. This town's no place to hide any more. It's all over.'

'Just start walkin' towards me, Leach,' Cleve said. 'I don't want to miss when I finish the job I sent Luke Trey to do.'

'What're you going to do after that? Kill Molly?' Nat started moving forward slowly until he was within three yards of the other man. 'You're an old hand at killing women, aren't you, Taggart? Didn't hesitate to kill my sister and my ma after you and the others violated them, did you?' Out of the corner of his eye, he saw a figure come round the corner at the end of the street, behind Taggart and his hostage.

'Save your breath, Leach,' Cleve said. 'You've. . . .'

'*Molly!*'

Toby Greenway took in the scene with mounting horror, but his shout was sufficient to make Cleve swing round and instinctively let loose a single shot from the rifle. The slug caught Toby in the shoulder and spun him sideways.

Molly screamed a second time. Nat raced forward and pulled her from Cleve's loosened grasp, then swung his fist with full force against the side of the other man's head. As Cleve went down, Nat tried to wrestle the Winchester free of his grasp, but Cleve hung on and the two men ended up rolling on the ground, locked together with the weapon between them.

155

Molly stood frozen to the spot, watching them. Toby staggered towards her and wrapped his arms around her, the blood seeping from his shoulder staining the front of her cornflower-coloured dress.

Suddenly, a muffled shot came from the rifle and the two men on the ground rolled apart.

Only one of them got to his feet.

Cleve Connor/Jess Taggart lay still, a bloody hole in his neck and under his chin. His eyes stared glassily at the sky.

CHAPTER 21

'Have you wired your friend Bud to tell him that his suspicions were correct?' Nat asked.

'Not yet,' Gabe said.

The two men were sitting with Angie at a quiet table in the corner of the dining room in Nat's hotel, a large pot of coffee between them. It was mid-morning, and two days since the confrontation with Lyle Walker, also known as Martin Benson, and the death of Cleve Connor, also known as Jess Taggart.

'What's stopping you?' Angie said.

'I'm trying to figure what it would achieve,' Gabe said. 'Benson's wife is still alive, and from what I can understand from Bud's wire, she has remarried.'

'So the marriage wouldn't be legal,' Nat said. 'Any more than Jane Walker's marriage to the man she knew as Lyle Walker was legal.'

'Exactly,' Gabe said. 'But Jane Brownlow – as she insists she's going to call herself again – assures me she doesn't plan to spread it around that her marriage was bigamous, and she's begged me to keep quiet about it.'

'Makes a kinda sense, I guess,' Nat said. 'But Bud Weston will be expecting *some* sort of explanation about what happened.'

'Yep, and he's not the sort of man to have the wool pulled over his eyes and not suspect something,' Gabe agreed. 'No, I think I'll write him a long letter instead of sending a wire. Tell him everything, including about the killing of your mother and sister and how you tracked down the perpetrators, if that's OK with you, Nat.'

Nat shrugged. 'It's OK.'

'And when I've done that, I'll suggest we leave the accepted version of the Stokewood murder to continue to be believed,' Gabe said. 'Let sleeping dogs lie.'

'You will?' Angie looked at him in surprise. 'That's not like you, Gabe, allowing the truth to go unreported.'

'I know, I know!' Gabe said. 'And it goes against my newspaperman's instincts. But what would be gained? The dead man, Jabal Hawley, was no saint, apparently. Nobody would be mourning his death if they learned he had been the victim in the fire at the real estate office. And we now know Martin Benson was the killer and, as Lyle Walker, ordered the murder of both Joe Spearing and Cliff Jarvis.'

'So we're shedding no tears over his death,' Angie said. 'Well, I never liked the man, and he would've made a terrible mayor.'

Gabe chuckled. 'Yes, well, that's one way of looking at it.'

'You reckon your old friend will go along with what you're suggesting?' Nat asked.

'I reckon he will,' Gabe said. He grinned. 'After he's got over the disappointment of missing a scoop for his paper.'

'What are you going to report about the deaths of Connor and Walker in your paper?' Nat said. 'Folks'll want some sort of explanation?'

'Same as I told Chap Fancy. That Lyle Walker must've known something Connor didn't want exposed. Everybody knows Cleve was as dangerous as a rabid dog when he felt threatened. And with Luke Trey dead, he had to do his own dirty work.'

'And Chap believed it?'

'Probably not. But he thought it best not to ask questions.'

Angie poured fresh coffee into their mugs. 'How's Toby?'

'He's gonna be fine,' Gabe said. 'The doc patched him up and he's enjoying the attention and sympathy he's getting from Molly Brownlow.'

'And Jane Brownlow?' Nat asked.

'Jane's tougher than she looks. She'll get over this, especially having Molly to help her.'

'How much did she know about all this?' Nat asked. 'Did she tell you?'

'She knew Lyle had a secret past, but no details,' Gabe said. 'I guess she preferred not to know. But then she overheard part of the conversation Joe Spearing had with her husband and the mention of Stokewood. She confronted him about it, but he convinced her to keep the conversation to herself. Then when Joe was murdered, she had her suspicions. But again, she refused to accept what seemed obvious. Went into denial, I guess you'd say.'

'How much does Molly know now?' Angie asked.

'Everything her ma knows,' Gabe said. 'Jane deemed it

wise not to try and hide anything from her daughter. I reckon that was sensible. Secrets are usually a bad thing. And they get found out, most often.'

'As both Connor and Walker discovered,' Nat said.

'Right,' Gabe said. 'Like a few other folk I could mention, they came here hoping to keep their secrets hidden.'

'Even a small out-of-the-way town like Ox Crossing is no place to hide when people are determined to learn the truth,' Nat said.

Gabe nodded. 'You're right, of course.

They drank their coffee in silence for several minutes, then Nat said, 'I'll be moving on tomorrow.'

'Going where?' Gabe said. 'Because, you know, folks would be happy for you to stay and put some roots down here. Drifting can be a lonesome way of living, Nat.'

'And this town needs a new sheriff,' Angie said. 'Chap's getting too old and tired to do the job properly.'

'I plan to go home,' Nat said. 'The farm where my ma and sister were living is still there, and it belongs to me. Sure, it's run down and will take a lot of work to bring it back to life, but I reckon it's something I'll take some pleasure in doing.'

'You a farmer!' Angie said, laughing.

'What's so funny?' Nat answered, grinning.

'Nothing, I guess,' she admitted.

'It's an honest living,' Gabe said. 'And if things don't work out, you know you'll be welcome here.'

'They'll work out,' Nat said. 'I'll make them.'

Gabe studied him for a moment. 'Guess you will at that,' he said.